THE BILLIONAIRE'S SEXY RIVAL

JAMESON BROTHERS BOOK THREE

LESLIE NORTH

CONTENTS

JAMESON BROTHERS

The Billionaire's Ex-Wife

The Billionaire's Pregnant Fling

The Billionaire's Sexy Rival

The BILLIONAIRE'S
Sexy Rival

USA TODAY BESTSELLING AUTHOR
LESLIE NORTH

BLURB

He wants to beat out the competition. But he never imagined the competition would be so tempting...

William Jameson is a born leader. Strong, efficient, and with a special talent for knowing exactly what turns people on—it's no surprise that he's the CEO of the billion-dollar Jameson Ad Agency. He's always had his choice of client—that is until a boutique agency called Wildflower sprouts up like a weed in his perfectly manicured world, stealing the last three jobs out from under him. It's hard not to be attracted to the free-spirited owner. Her mind and body are exactly what his heart wants...it's too bad his goal is to crush her as competition.

Poppy Hanniford, CEO of the Wildflower Agency, has always been unique and as colorful as her business's name. A fan of communal collaboration and out of the box ideas, Poppy and William come together in the perfect storm when a rogue romance publisher decides that two is sometimes better than one: challenging Poppy and William to work together on a trial project. The person who performs best, wins their future business.

Forced by the client into teaming up, William and Poppy are about to find that while their leadership styles don't mix, romance is one subject they agree on. A smoldering kiss for the cover of a book kicks off an affair that's hotter than the best-sellers they want to advertise. When it's made clear that only one of them can walk away with the contract, they'll need to decide what's more important: the job or their love.

MAILING LIST

Thank you for purchasing 'The Billionaire's Sexy Rival'
(Jameson Brothers Book Three)

**Get SIX full-length novellas by USA Today best-selling
author Leslie North for FREE! Over 548 pages of best-selling
romance with a combined 1133 FIVE STAR REVIEWS!**

Sign-up to her mailing list and get your FREE books at:
http://leslienorthbooks.com/sign-up-for-free-books

ABOUT LESLIE

Leslie North is the USA Today Bestselling pen name for a critically-acclaimed author of women's contemporary romance and fiction. The anonymity gives her the perfect opportunity to paint with her full artistic palette, especially in the romance and erotic fantasy genres.

To discover more about Leslie North visit:

LeslieNorthBooks.com

Facebook: fb.com/leslienorthbooks

Twitter: @leslienorthbook

Goodreads: Goodreads.com/author/show/1899287.Leslie_North

Bookbub: Bookbub.com/authors/leslie-north

CHAPTER ONE

WILLIAM

The clock on the wall read five minutes to three. William Jameson could see it clearly from where he sat. It hung just above the head of the CEO of Wildflower Agency, Poppy Hanniford, who sat across from him in the waiting area, her long legs crossed and one ankle wagging along with the music the secretary played at her desk.

William Jameson kept himself still. He kept his eyes trained forward, and his broad hands laced in his lap over the paper copy of his proposal. Poppy had brought an identical folder with her; it rested on the low end table beside her.

He watched his rival without ever making eye contact, or giving the appearance of watching anything in particular. Poppy was less practiced at pretending not to watch him in return. A minute or so would pass, and she would glance across the room, as if to check if anything in his stony demeanor had changed. William remained inflexible.

He recognized her, of course, from her own agency's promotional materials, and from glimpses across the New York mixers they had both attended in the past. They had never met officially, and neither of them had ever gone out of their way to initiate a proper introduction. The closest he had ever come to direct contact with Poppy Hanniford was watching her steal three accounts out from under him.

Three. That was three too many, and he was determined that there be no fourth.

Love Connection Publishing had invited them both in today for a joint interview. When William was informed that Wildflower Agency had agreed to the terms, he had likewise come onboard. It was unusual for clients to request simultaneous pitches from two agencies at once, but William had no problem rising to the challenge. He allowed himself to feel coolly impressed that Poppy hadn't backed down, either—then again, he would expect nothing less from the CEO of his agency's most formidable rival.

Why *had* he even agreed to this interview? The Jameson Agency didn't need this account. In fact, they were swimming in projects already—something Trinity, his sister-in-law and one of his top employees, had been all too happy to remind him of. Repeatedly. Their staff and resources were already stretched thin from coast to coast, not to mention preoccupied with building clientele overseas; it was a good and prosperous thing to be so inundated with work, with more potential clients eagerly hammering on their door.

But damn it, William didn't want to lose to Poppy Hanniford

and her hippy-dippy agency again. If his reputation wasn't at stake, then his ego certainly was. And if this trend of losing kept up, he wasn't certain it *wouldn't* affect his family business. Curious clients might start turning their heads.

Not that he could blame them.

William decided to change tack now. He sized Poppy up in the hope of making her feel a bit more intimidated than her quiet grooving implied. He let his eyes linger obviously on her jouncing leg; her feminine figure; her long blonde hair and youthful face. He knew she wasn't many years younger than him, but she could have passed for twenty with the heels and fiery red lipstick. He couldn't fathom how she had managed to take those accounts from him. In every situation he exuded calm, authoritativeness, maturity. He upheld a reputation in New York that had been established three generations ago. Jameson Advertising Agency was old, and respected, and *venerated*. It was a fixture. What the businesses of New York wanted was a clear history of leadership and a pronounced willingness to win. *History* was what his agency had to offer that Wildflower did not; hell, even the name 'Jameson' trumped the whimsy of her floral appellation, and he had arrived at that opinion completely objectively as an ad man. And as for winning? He had only postponed it in this case. Now, he knew he couldn't afford to ignore Wildflower any longer. He would lead his agency to victory, and put that upstart Poppy Hanniford in her place: that is to say, *second.*

Who named their child *Poppy,* anyway?

The name was cute, even lovely in its own way—certainly as lovely as the woman who answered to it—and utterly misleading. Like a flower, the eye-catching Poppy had sprouted up out of nowhere, but she was no gentle specimen. She was a thorn in his side, utterly unpluckable despite his best efforts, but maybe it was time for the gloves to come off. He wanted this account. He would *have* this account—and his obsession with the gorgeous, leg-swinging, glance-casting woman sitting across from him would end alongside his victory.

All he had to do was command the presentation room marginally better than he was commanding this one.

His phone buzzed in his back pocket, and he shifted slightly-- his first mistake of the day. The proposal slipped from his lap and slid across the carpet between them. It came to a stop in front of Poppy Hanniford.

The jogging ankle froze.

William half-rose in his chair, but Poppy picked his folder up in one smooth movement. It fell open in her hands, exposing the mock-up of the first splash page. "Oh. This is really good," she said.

William blinked.

"Your social media spot," Poppy unpacked unnecessarily. "It's far and away better than mine." She cast a longing glance toward her own folder, as if she could see right through it to a design she found wanting. "I'm still going to pitch, but I really think you're a shoo-in for the account this time."

"You think so?" he asked drily. He wasn't sure what game she was playing, but he allowed himself to relax back into his chair, as if having his folder in enemy hands wasn't any cause for concern... and as if her off-handed *this time* hadn't rankled him in the slightest. The chessboard was getting interesting now that Poppy had made her first move.

"Do you mind?" Poppy held up his proposal, and William nodded an invitation. She flipped through it quickly, nodding to herself with every page. She rose before she had even reached the end and sidled over to the chair beside him; William adjusted himself unnecessarily. In rooms this small, he always felt he took up more room than he should physically. Poppy didn't appear to notice as she sat down.

"This is excellent work," she continued. "Really, really excellent. Did you do this yourself?"

"I gave my input." William steepled his fingers as he watched her go over it all again from the beginning. "It doesn't matter if the account is big or small: nothing leaves our offices without my final approval." *On any coast,* he appended privately, and a little proudly, although he didn't think it necessary to further remark on his involvement.

Poppy flipped back to a page she kept getting hung up on. She squinted. Her eyes were a rare green, William noticed; it was only upon closer examination that he saw them clearly. Her headshot, though lovely, didn't do her justice. She was an extraordinarily beautiful woman when experienced in three dimenions.

"You know what would make it even better?" Poppy tapped her index finger meditatively against her lower lip as she spoke. William would have found the gesture infinitely more distracting if her words didn't get his hackles up in an instant. "What would really make it *pop?"* she continued, perhaps after sensing her assertion could be taken the wrong way.

…but William refused to let any criticism, uninvited or otherwise, disturb his outward peace and calm. He had deliberately worked to project himself as a lordly presence in the room, and he wasn't about to let the little flower bloom large enough to soak up his sun. "What would make it 'pop', exactly?" he asked her.

The finger continued to tap the plump, dark red flesh of her lip. William wondered if it was some sort of trick Poppy had picked to lull her male competition into complacency; whatever it was, he refused to fall victim to it. He had been doing this for far too long to be struggling against such charms now. When the finger came away, it rose toward the ceiling as if to punctuate a sudden thought. Poppy fished around her purse and pulled out a compact.

"Purple highlights." She sounded so confident in her suggestion that William didn't second-guess how she knew. "That's what the title needs. Your font choice is impeccable, but a shadow will really make it stand out without being too obnoxiously intrusive." She flipped the compact open to show him a pallet of shimmering violet powder. *Eye shadow,* William realized.

"Hmmm." He mulled over her words as he squinted down at the title of his media spot. "You know, I think you're right." He reached for the compact to apply the shadow himself, but Poppy drew it out of his reach and shook her head.

"Please. Allow me. I promise I have more practice with the application process." She beamed so wide her eyes partially closed, and it was the sweetest, most genuine smile that William had ever seen... and he saw a *lot* of smiles in his line of work, genuine and otherwise.

"That smile pushes products and steals clients," he noted, as if there had ever been any question. Poppy laughed appreciatively as he passed his proposal to her. He was glad to see that she had taken his words as the compliment they were meant to be. "If you weren't my rival, I would put you on a billboard."

"Thank you, Mr. Jameson. I admit those are more flattering words than I expected from you."

"Do you do this with all your proposals?" he inquired as he craned across the arm of his chair to watch her work. Now that the presentation was out of his hands, he was genuinely nervous, although years of experience enabled him to hide the fact. Still, what if she sabotaged him now? He would have no one to blame but himself.

Poppy shook her head. It was a pretty gesture, and William liked the way her shimmering spill of blonde hair fell around her shoulders. Another tactic? She engaged with him so naturally he thought he probably wasted his energy looking for an underhanded motive in everything she did. "No. I usually save the makeup for my face."

You don't need any, he was tempted to say. He held his tongue. "Not many people would think of purple," he observed as she dabbed along the sides of each letter. "I certainly wouldn't."

"It hardly matters," Poppy offered offhand. "Your entire presentation is far and away better than what I brought with me." She spoke with such conviction that William drew back a little to get another look at her. He had never sat through a rival lavishing praise on him before… then again, Poppy wasn't 'lavishing' so much as she appeared to think she really was identifying a superior product. "I'm still working to find a place for this one former intern." She glanced mournfully at her own proposal, neglected and still sitting on the table across the room. "He's an emo kid, and he's *constantly* on social media. I really thought he'd nail this one." She sighed.

"I thought emo kids went extinct in the early 2000s," William said.

Poppy chuckled. "He has a good heart. I really would like to find him a permanent place at Wildflower… I just think he's maybe less cut out for design than his extreme penchant for personal grooming had led me to believe. There." She finished her adjustment with a flourish and passed the folder back to William. "That's better, don't you think?"

"I think you're right," he replied. The social media spot looked miles better than it had when he first walked through the front doors of the publishing house. Why hadn't anyone on his team thought of this? Didn't he take pains to acquire—and hire— the very best in the business, just like his father and grandfather before him?

Poppy grinned. "You're going to do great in there. It really is an awesome piece of media." She took her makeup brush, twiddled it once more in the eyeshadow, and began to apply the shimmer to her upper lids. William watched her, fascinated. He knew his guard was down, and yet he couldn't help it…and anyway, he was confident that Poppy wouldn't notice him looking at her keenly in her present pursuit.

He needed to say something. He knew this, and yet the harder he racked his brain, the harder to come up with something appropriate given the circumstances. Did he offer her advice on her own proposal? Did he wish her luck in return? Every option sounded absurd, and yet…it hadn't rung wrong, or false, when Poppy did it.

"Mr. Jameson? Ms. Hanniford?"

William glanced up, and Poppy's compact snapped shut. The secretary stood in the doorway to the boardroom, hands laced, wearing an expectant smile.

"They're ready for your presentations now. If you'll follow me?"

CHAPTER TWO

POPPY

The room was like any other New York boardroom Poppy Hanniford had seen: boxy, with a forced air of personality that didn't quite escape past the two-dimensional motivational posters and recycled, misattributed quotes that papered the walls. At least the side of the room that looked out toward the cityscape was a floor-to-ceiling window; this, too, was typical, but she never found the view of the bejeweled skyscrapers and distant harbor any less breathtaking. A plate of miniature muffins steamed on a plate positioned in the dead center of the table, hopelessly out of reach of anyone who might dare to think they were intended for consumption.

She knew the room. She knew the script. She knew her presentation backwards and forwards—the only difference was this time, she *also* knew she was going to lose the contract.

And she was strangely okay with it.

She cut a quick sideways glance at William as they both

migrated toward the front of the room. He was exchanging pleas-
antries, and she was doing the same, shaking hands and watching
him all the while. The photos she saw of him around the subway
—not to mention the splash pages in magazines showcasing his
opulent life outside of the office—really didn't do the man
justice. The way he carried himself, you'd think he rolled out of
his California King every morning with his dark hair perfectly
coiffed; the shadow of his stubble perfectly maintained; the
dimples...

Oh lord, the dimples. Did they Photoshop them out of all his
professional photos? William didn't smile often, but when his
generous lips did flex in the vague direction of mirth, his stern
jaw gave way to a perfectly symmetrical pair of dimples. They
made his cheekbones more defined, his dark, almond-shaped
eyes more curved and crinkled. Up close, he was a completely
irresistible specimen of a human being.

And he definitely knew it.

"Ms. Hanniford? Would you like to start us off?"

Poppy blinked slowly to disguise the fact that she needed to
mentally come back down to earth. Several potential clients had
that look of expectation in their eyes, and she nodded. She knew
what was being asked of her without having been present the last
several seconds. William watched her, and one of his dimples
resurfaced; he looked distinctly amused. Poppy wondered if he
could see past her mask of calm.

She nodded and moved to the front of the room. The others
took their seats; William remained standing. He leaned back
against her side of the table and crossed his arms. Poppy

wondered if he knew just how distracting his impressive fore-arms were. She cleared her throat.

"I just want to take a quick moment to thank you for the opportunity you've extended to Wildflower Agency," she began. "I speak for everyone back at my office when I say just how excited I am to be here today." She spoke her introduction easily, confidently. She saw the stiff bodies inside the little boardroom begin to relax as she massaged them with her pitch.

"...and I have here a mockup of what the social media spot would look like, if you'll turn your attention to the board your lovely secretary is wheeling in..."

Poppy continued an explanation of her vision—more accurately, her intern's amateur bastardization of her vision—as she called attention to points of interest in the larger-than-life graphics she had brought with her. She preferred tangible presentation elements to projections or PowerPoints. She could see her audience nodding along, and better yet, leaning in to discuss with their neighbors as she carried on.

"...that being said, I think the ideas that the Jameson Ad Agency has brought with them today would result in a superior product," she concluded. "I'm happy to give the floor up now and segue into Mr. Jameson's presentation."

A surprised murmur rippled through the boardroom. William, for once, looked completely thrown off his game. She could see it in the clench of his hands gripping the conference table. He was very good at hiding his reaction, but Poppy knew the signs. She often surprised people the way she had just surprised William. And it wasn't just some tactic to undermine his calm—no matter what his puzzled gaze quietly accused her of.

Poppy motioned to the empty spot beside her. After a moment's consideration, William pushed off from the table to join her at the front of the room. He was an intelligent man. He would take the opportunity given to him. Poppy sidestepped to allow him the floor.

"Jumping off from what Miss Hanniford was saying, I find her approach well-considered, and her reasoning completely sound. With that in mind..." William flowed dazzlingly into his own idea for the media spot, as if he needed no introduction, and no segue was required. Poppy couldn't help but watch admiringly; his hands swept the air, he held his audience with his gaze...until that gaze slid her way.

"...something like that, Miss Hanniford?"

"I couldn't have said it better myself, Mr. Jameson." She meant it, and she let her agreement show in her smile. Was it her imagination, or did William lean toward her then, just a little? It was hard to tell where her presentation ended, and his began... and it was harder still to track their distance from one another when her full attention was completely caught up in him.

"Wonderful!"

Poppy blinked and turned from William back to their audience. The head of Love Connection Publishing rose from her chair and offered a small, singular applause; judging by the looks exchanged by the others at the table, this sort of reception had never happened in the boardroom before.

"I want you. Both of you," the head emphasized, her eyes

tracking between them. "We're going to proceed with the interview process, but I want the two of you working together every step of the way."

Poppy exchanged looks with William. "This is highly unorthodox..." William said, but he appeared at a loss. Poppy had to privately agree with him, although she wondered at the dismay in his tone. It was as if the client had personally insulted him with her indecision. Poppy herself had been under the impression that today's presentation would be the deciding factor when it came to which agency the publishing house wanted representing it. She had thought Jameson Agency would win the deal with their pitch.

But she didn't betray her puzzlement now as much as William did. Whatever his problem was, she could use it to her advantage to look like the bigger man...so to speak. She turned back to the head of the house, smiling gamely. "All right. So a collaboration going forward between agencies is what you have in mind?"

The publisher nodded. "I can only see good things resulting from the *tete-a-tete* the two of you engaged in today. If you accept my offer, the two of you will be working together with the panel of authors I have lined up for Conventional Romance this year. The person who works most successfully with the members of our panel, and helps our authors to successfully create and present materials to promote Love Connection at the con, will be the one awarded the account."

Poppy nodded. "Conventional Romance" was the biggest annual romance writers' convention to appear in New York City, if not the entire country, and the press coverage of the event was only ramping up with each passing year. *Conventions* were getting airtime, as was the motley assortment of content creators, cosplay fans, and fringe enthusiasts who attended them with such devotion and vigor. It was an incredible opportunity to promote her client, not to mention her own business—even if she did have to share the opportunity with her agency's biggest rival.

"And how will the interview process be judged going forward?" William asked.

"I'm so glad you asked." The publisher came around to their side of the table and leaned back, crossing her arms over her chest. She appeared to be sizing William up over the trendy frames of her glasses—not as a sexually interested woman sizes up a man, Poppy thought, but as a writer sizes up a potential muse. It amused Poppy to think that a hero of William's description might soon be appearing between the covers of a steamy romance novel. "Your performance will be judged on how well you work within the author group. I'm excited to see which one of you pulls out all the stops and brings the most to the table for my house and its writers."

Is it just me, or did she emphasize the word 'performance'? Poppy mastered a wicked grin at William's expense. She had to hand it to him, if he was at all uncomfortable being pinned by the needle-sharp gaze of this professional woman, he hid it well.

"I assure everyone in this boardroom that Jameson Agency won't let you down," William said.

"Wildflower Agency blooms beautifully under pressure," Poppy agreed with a grin. She knew her audience, and could tell that they approved of her metaphor.

"Excellent. I look forward to seeing what the two of you come up with." The publisher took turns shaking hands with the two of them, before motioning for them to exit at their leisure. Poppy gathered up her documents, then leaned across the table to help herself to one of the muffins. When she straightened, she noticed William's dark eyes burning into her. She couldn't tell what he was thinking when he looked at her like that—all she knew was she felt the intensity in his gaze in the pit of her stomach, and possibly lower...

But it was no use trying to mind-read someone like William. He may look mild-mannered and distinguished on the outside, but Poppy knew there was more going on below the surface. Beneath still waters a shark-churned current roiled.

He held the door for her on their way out. Poppy accepted the gesture, taking a bite off the top of her muffin as if she hadn't even noticed. William followed after.

"Well, that was interesting," he muttered as soon as they were out in the hallway.

"I agree," she replied. "But that's how I like to keep my life: interesting. Unpredictable."

"I think you've succeeded," he said. "Even if it's at the immediate expense of clinching your client."

"Oh, I'm not worried." Poppy took another dismissive bite of her muffin. She *was* worried. She wanted so badly to add the publishing house to her roster, but William and his agency were proving to be stiff competition already. He had learned a thing or two from tangling with her in the past, and understood now that she wasn't to be overlooked. *Even old agency dogs can learn new tricks*...not that William was particularly old, but he was CEO of an agency that had been established long before either of them were born. "Only they can decide what's best for them," she added.

"I find that an extremely interesting, if misguided, approach to take." William held his hand out to her. Poppy didn't allow herself a split second's hesitation. She grasped it, knowing full well what was coming.

The pressure of his handshake was instantaneous: his grip was powerful, his fingers and palm contracting together to dwarf her. Poppy had never been so aware of the petite size of her own hands than she was in that moment. Still, it was a power play she was all too familiar with, and she wasn't about to back down just because William might be physically stronger than she was. She tightened her fingers and clutched him back with all her might. She saw one of William's dimples leap approvingly into prominence.

"Congratulations on winning the first round, Mr. Jameson," she said.

He crooked a dark, perfectly-maintained eyebrow at her. "I beg your pardon?"

"You didn't think you'd won the war, did you? Just because I promoted your design over my own?" Poppy let the smile bloom across her face slowly, drawing her painted lips back over what she knew to be a set of immaculate, pristine white teeth. She wanted to dazzle him as much as she suddenly wanted to demolish him. William may wind up coming out on top when all was said and done, but that didn't mean she couldn't give it all she had. She would fight fairly for this contract, but she would fight.

"I wasn't aware that we were at war, Miss Hanniford," William remarked. "And if we are, I certainly don't expect my enemy to concede to me as easily as you did today. It shows a lack of strong leadership, to the employees that depend on you for a paycheck…and to me."

The hand that held hers tightened. Their arms no longer moved in the up and down rhythm that made a handshake. Poppy gazed unflinchingly into William's deep, dark eyes.

"I concede when I know I am beaten," she replied icily. "And I'm not often beaten. I would think you and your agency know that better than anyone, Mr. Jameson." She extracted her hand from his; at the last instant, when she thought he wouldn't let her go, he allowed her to slip free. Her skin tingled with the memory of his grip. Poppy hoped it wasn't a sign of nerve damage.

She hoped the tingling didn't signal something *else,* either.

"Good day, Mr. Jameson."

"Good day, Miss Hanniford."

They parted ways coolly, in stark contrast to Poppy's skin, which still burned fever-hot hours later where William Jameson had touched her.

CHAPTER THREE

WILLIAM

William never thought the day would come that he would see his younger brother Sam boasting a tan. Eddie had always been the outdoorsman of the three of them, but even William managed to see enough sun to give himself some healthy color. In the past, Sam had always appeared as icy on the outside as his personality and business dealings were within. He never used to leave the office if he could help it, and his skin had been an almost vampiric white.

Such was not the case now. Now that he was back with Trinity, Sam had thawed—and the couples' time together working in Australia had outwardly tanned them beyond recognition. If William found the look jarring on his brother, it certainly benefited Trinity; she positively glowed, from within and without.

"Wow. So you're really taking this individual pitch personally, huh?" she asked him now.

The three of them were holding an impromptu meeting over

instant coffee in one of the Jameson boardrooms. William had briefed the two of them on his presentation to the publishing house; he had hoped to breeze past it as just another business update, but Trinity's sudden laser-focus was making it difficult for him to move onto other topics.

"It's unlike you," Sam noted. As if Sam was in any position to point out other people not acting like themselves these days. William fixed him with a critical look, but his brother seemed unfazed. At least that much hadn't changed.

"You're not usually so hands-on," Trinity continued. "What's so different about this one, William? You're the CEO. Why don't you just delegate?"

Why don't you just delegate? "Because Poppy Hanniford didn't delegate," William said. True, she may have given one of her underlings a chance to flex their design ideas in the first round—a mistake that should have cost her the running—but she had shown up, and taken personal responsibility for the product her agency put out. Not only that, she had highlighted her own weakness quite *winningly.* Even William couldn't deny how endearing, how *appealing,* her bald-faced sincerity had come across. It was unlike anything he had ever encountered in the business, and he had spent most of his life learning the negotiation techniques and counter-attacks required to send his rivals packing.

No, this prospective client required a personal touch. *His* personal touch. It was time for Poppy Hanniford to see firsthand just how formidable he was.

"I prefer that a Jameson represent Jameson Agency in this

case," William continued. "And with the two of you in Australia and Eddie on paternity leave, that leaves only me."

"Seems like you're on the fast track to winning the contract with your one-man show," Trinity observed. "Or at least you *were* on-track—until you let Poppy Hanniford get under your skin."

William opened his mouth to argue. He wasn't a man who normally allowed himself to get into conversations where he had to play defense. At the last minute, he caught the sly look in Trinity's eye, and clamped his mouth closed. Any protest he could form—and he could think of a hundred different ones he might throw her way—would only confirm...*whatever it was* that she was thinking.

"You spin narratives as expertly as the authors I'm tasked with wrangling," William said.

"Don't you mean the authors you and *Poppy* are tasked with wrangling?" Trinity smirked.

Sam glanced between them. He crossed his arms. He was less quick picking up on the undercurrent of the conversation, but now looked as if he had noticed enough to come along for the ride.

"There's no way Jameson is going to lose this client to Wildflower," William said confidently. "The right track you perceived us following before is the same one we're on now."

"Jameson Agency has always been a family business," Trinity said. She sat back, tapping her pen, and dropped a glance in Sam's direction. "...but it's only recently that you guys really started to come together and show the world—and yourselves—

that the best way to succeed is to put family first. You've finally made your interpersonal relationships the focus, and the business has only profited from it. I'm just afraid of seeing all your hard work fall by the wayside if you choose to make this your number one priority. You've already cancelled meetings with Eddie multiple times these past few weeks. He'd never admit it, but he was really looking forward to spending time with you. I just don't want to see you put your family second again."

"You're wrong," William said dismissively. "I appreciate your take as always, Trinity, but putting the business first *is* putting family first. It's a family business, as the name implies."

"But that doesn't mean there has to be a patriarch!" Trinity said in exasperation. "You don't have to rule everything with an iron fist, William!"

"Trinity." Sam's voice took a tone of warning, but William put his hand up.

"Please, Samson. Let her finish. I meant it when I said I value her unfiltered input."

"It's just…" Trinity glanced between the two of them, her determined expression folding into concern, "…all three of you brothers work so well together. As a *team.* I'm afraid all the emphasis on taking down Wildflower sounds more like a personal vendetta, William. That's all."

"I will take that into consideration," he promised. "Now Sam, if you'd excuse us…there is something I'd like Trinity to look over for me."

"I owe Eddie a phone call, anyway," Sam said as he rose. "I'll be sure to send him your love."

William waved him off. He was already deep in contemplation concerning the next order of business. Trinity rose to come around to his side of the table and examine the documents he spread before him.

"Is this your business plan for the romance convention?" she asked curiously. William nodded, taking a step back to grant her full access to his outline. "Wow. You've really thought of everything, haven't you?"

"Exercising that iron fist," he agreed. "I know you've been highly successful in the past running many of our all-female production groups out of L.A. I just wanted your opinion on my plan before I push forward."

"My opinion?" Trinity turned to him, and William guessed what was coming. Thankfully, he hadn't gotten this far by throwing up walls every time he was faced with outside criticism. "Your 'iron fist' is what's going to get you into trouble. Not just with running the business, and running the family—which you *claim* to be one and the same—but with this project. In my experience, female-dominated companies don't respond well to the 'man in charge' angle. Even the ones who make a fortune publishing BDSM," Trinity said as an afterthought to herself.

"But I am the man in charge," William pointed out. "By inviting me to continue with them, they've effectively *put* me in charge. It's what they're paying for, Trinity."

Trinity shook her head. "They're paying for your unique perspective,…but what *none* of those women will find unique is some alpha male New York CEO trying to tell them what's best for them. And anyway, need I remind you, you're *not* the one in charge. Even if the two of you are locked in competition for the contract, you still agreed to share responsibilities with Poppy Hanniford. You think she's going to let you walk all over her?"

She might. William doubted if Trinity had ever met Poppy in person, much less found herself on the end of the other woman's cheerleading. It was an exercise in self-defeat… but then why did he always wind up *losing* to her?

He couldn't get her out of his head. Trinity was right: Poppy Hanniford was in his mind and under his skin. Maybe that was exactly what the woman had intended all along…maybe she played the game by a set of rules that even William, in all his years as an ad exec, hadn't had the chance to learn. Not yet, anyway.

But he would learn. He would watch Poppy like a hawk. He would let his eyes linger on her curves; her lush mouth; her scented sweep of hair. He would let her know in the space of a disinterested glance just how disinterested he was in her win-by-losing tactic—regardless of the fact that he couldn't figure out how she had even managed it in the first place. By every law he and the rest of the sensible world subscribed to, a person shouldn't tie in any competition by throwing the game. He would get to the bottom of her act and expose it for what he was certain it was: a new spin on an old tactic. He just didn't know which tactic yet.

But he intended to find out.

"William? Are you sure you're all right?" Trinity was looking at him. The wryly amused expression she had worn for most of their meeting gave way to one of thoughtful concern.

William leaned against the table and took a bland sip of his coffee. "Of course. Never better. Why do you ask?"

Trinity just shook her head. "You know, for a brother-in-law who professes to weigh everything I tell him, you really don't like it when I tell you you're making a mistake."

"Am I making a mistake?" The word may as well have existed in a foreign language for all the times it had been relevant to his life. William set his Styrofoam cup down and straightened his tie. "What I think I'm making is a play to win."

"The agency wins all the time" Trinity pointed out. "If I didn't know any better, I'd say you just want to see Wildflower Agency lose."

I want to see Poppy Hanniford lose, William thought.

He didn't know why, but making the unflappable blonde writhe was foremost on his mind.

CHAPTER FOUR

POPPY

Poppy stared at the huge wooden desk in wonder. She had never seen a piece of furniture so mighty. It hulked like a mythical four-legged beast before her, crouched and ready to pounce should any trespasser attempt to leave a meeting unexcused. It seemed like everyone assembled was deliberately ignoring it, but there it was.

William Jameson sat enshrined behind it. His presence wasn't dwarfed by his desk, but rather he seemed to loom even larger and more formidably for it, like a king at his dais in the receiving room.

It was on the tip of Poppy's tongue to make some clever remark about his choice of furniture, but she kept it to herself. The desk *was* overkill, but that didn't mean it didn't suit the man, the office, the...*everything*. It seemed way too ancient for him, though. She wondered if it was a holdover from the time when his father, or even his grandfather, lorded over Jameson Ad Agency in his place.

Anyway, she didn't like to imagine that William Jameson had anything to compensate for. Not that she made it a *habit* of imagining William at all, especially not in the recent days since meeting him. Still, it would serve him right if she called his prowess into question now. She couldn't imagine that his insistence on holding the meeting in his office was anything more than a power play.

And she was determined to get out ahead of it.

So this is how the other half lives, Poppy thought as she took a turn about the room. Jameson Agency benefited from its history; Wildflower from its moxie and innovation. They were bound to find out by the end of all this which was the best side of the coin to be on.

"What do you think of my domain, Miss Hanniford?"

Poppy almost jumped, but managed to play it cool at the last second. William had risen from his desk to come up behind her while she was preoccupied. She glanced sidelong at him as he stood behind her, gazing out at the same cityscape she was drinking in. She doubted it interested him as much as he pretended. This latest maneuver was all about *her,* and she was well aware of it. Hard to ignore the way he stood at her back.

"'Domain' is certainly the word I would use," she agreed. She didn't turn, or give ground. Defying all laws of personal space, William stepped closer to her. Every nerve screamed with awareness of him. The fine hairs on the back of her neck stood on end, as if straining toward the electricity that sizzled between them.

"I like to take ownership of my surroundings," William replied. "Don't you?"

"Playing for the away team never slowed me down before, Mr. Jameson. But I understand if some people aren't comfortable with it."

"Mr. Jameson? Ms. Hanniford?"

The two of them turned when called. One of the younger and more timid-looking authors on the panel held her hand up in apology. "Sorry to interrupt. We're ready to start brainstorming when you are."

Poppy nodded. The panel the publishing house had selected was larger than she expected. Seven authors total, plus herself and William, made even his enormous office feel overcrowded. It wasn't helping matters that she could sense the women's uncertainty. They probably hadn't expected to have to deal directly with two rival ad execs.

They all settled into the chairs that had been brought in for them. Poppy remained by the window, just off to the side of William, who had assumed a position at the head of the room. At least he hadn't sequestered himself back behind the desk. The optics of him ruling over the proceedings like a king definitely wouldn't have worked out well for them here.

"All right. Welcome, everyone." William led them off. "I'd like to get started right away in answering any questions or concerns you might have for me. *Us,*" he corrected quickly. Poppy wondered if the slip had been intentional; in either case, she couldn't resist letting her mouth quirk to betray her amusement. William was so obviously not used to playing with others, much less asking for their input.

The authors all looked at each other. Poppy felt as if she could read their minds. They didn't know whether this was a pleasantry on William's part or a genuine invitation. "Well, our panel is about how to take the traditional images of romance publishing and make them unique," one offered.

"Good," William responded.

Poppy nodded. "And what we're here for is to help you come up with a visual so absolutely explosive as to make our panel the one that attendees can't stop talking about, for *years* to come. That's exactly where all our heads should be at. We need to tap into the tropes that your readers have been conditioned to look for, but we also need to find a new spin to set our campaign apart. Does anyone have any suggestions?"

The authors all exchanged looks again. They looked a shy, introverted bunch, Poppy realized, but she thought she knew better. There had to be an undercurrent of edge here, otherwise they wouldn't all excel at what they did. She just had to find it and tap into it: it was a vein of gold.

William seemed less patient. He crossed his arms. "Anybody?" he prompted. "Come now. You can't have all come to this meeting unprepared."

Poppy's hackles rose on the authors' behalves. It was no use shaming or blaming this early in the meeting. She placed a hand on his bicep and stepped forward before she knew what she was doing. "I have an idea," she volunteered. "Beginning here. We'll design a romance cover—or at least, an image *evocative* of a romance cover. We'll put it on posters for the event, blow it up on banners—we'll place it everywhere a pair of eyes has the opportunity to see it."

The authors all exchanged looks. "Book covers aren't usually done that way," one offered.

"But it's every author's dream to have creative control of her own cover," another added. "What did you have in mind when you say 'beginning here', Miss Hanniford?"

"I want you guys to direct. And don't hold back on ideas." Poppy took an assessing glance at herself, then at William. She had a wild idea, but she wasn't sure how it would pay off... what she *really* hoped was to relieve some of the women's self-consciousness. She needed them to focus outside of themselves and think more creatively

To do that, Poppy decided, she just might have to make a spectacle of herself.

"Why don't you arrange the two of us in a sort of tableau?" she suggested. "I think we fit the average body types portrayed on your covers. Would that help you visualize better?"

William looked miffed at her accusation of 'average', although it certainly wasn't what she meant. He was tall, hunky, and probably *very* gym-sculpted beneath the suit—a man of his station and responsibilities, both professional and private, simply didn't let his own health fall by the wayside in her experience. He probably maintained a strict diet and exercise schedule; the results may have mostly been hidden, but she could still see it in the controlled, graceful way he moved. He was in perfect command of his body, just like he was in perfect command of his company.

"…that would help," one of the authors agreed.

"Oh, I like this idea," another said. She chatted enthusiastically with the woman sitting beside her, who nodded and blushed at something she said. This woman in particular was having a hard time making eye contact with William, or even really looking in his direction. She gave the impression of someone trying very hard not to stare directly into the sun.

"Great!" Poppy clapped her hands, then held her arms out to William.

"What?" he deadpanned. He didn't budge an inch.

"Dip me, Mr. Jameson," she said. "Time to put on a show."

She prodded him. He was as immobile as a statue…that, Poppy mused, or this was his natural state: rock-hard. Her teasing poke had loosened him up, though. It took some coaxing, but she finally managed to convince William to wrap his arms around her and hold her parallel to the floor. The position was awkward, but the authors were all talking now. Many of them looked dubious, but at least they weren't locked in painful silence.

"Or what if I sort of…" Poppy righted herself and pushed William's arms away, then draped herself in a sultry display over his shoulders. A chorus of disappointed sighs told her this was all wrong. It was a good response—it meant that the wheels were turning.

"We need props," someone suggested.

"Their bodies are the props. What we need is *setting*," another emphasized. "And set pieces!"

"The desk!"

There was a sudden clamor for the desk, and Poppy and William found themselves ushered over to it. Directions were given, and the two of them arranged themselves accordingly. William bent nearer, and placed his palms down flat on either side of her; Poppy lifted her hand to touch his cheek. His skin was warm, and rough, and so evocative of easy masculinity that she couldn't help losing herself in the moment for a second... only a second. The spicy aroma of his cologne washed over her. She forbade herself from breathing it in too deeply. It was probably formulated to be intoxicating to women.

"You have silver in your hair," she observed.

"Is that your way of implying that I'm old?"

"I think it's distinguished," Poppy replied, before another shouted suggestion had William flipping her and bending her over the desk. His crotch butted up against her ass. Poppy was certain her face must have been bright scarlet in this position—if it were a color in her favorite lipstick line, it would have been "Giveaway Red". But the tone of the room had shifted from mischievous to contemplative, and many of the women were taking furious notes and consulting one another. William politely held the pose for them. The hand that cradled her ribcage and forced her back to arch beneath him stroked her belly idly, and Poppy squirmed.

"Okay. We decided that position is a little too racy and impersonal," one of the authors said.

You think? Poppy wanted to cry out.

"What about this one?" To her surprise, it was William who offered the suggestion. He grabbed her waist and flipped her around so that she was angled back against the desk beneath him. Poppy quickly rearranged herself, then hiked one leg up and looked to her audience. Several of them gasped with happiness. They had just struck gold.

"Now sort of...thread your fingers though her hair," one of the authors instructed. William did. The pressure on Poppy's scalp made her whole head tingle. He didn't just abide by the placement, he actually *tugged,* and her head fell back a little. She looked up into his eyes. She wanted to smile to reassure him, but she couldn't remember how. His suddenly introspective look pulled her, and it was an alarming moment when she realized: *he doesn't need to be reassured.* He knew exactly what he was doing. It was only the circumstances surrounding the move that threw him off.

"Now kiss her," one of the authors, the one with her phone out, suggested. Poppy tried to turn her head in alarm, but William's fingers held her fast.

"What?" she squeaked.

"Please, Miss Hanniford, all the best-selling novels have kicked it up a notch in recent years." One author with thick-rimmed glasses spoke. She seemed totally untitillated by the whole affair. She must have been in this business a long time, Poppy realized. "It's not enough to be brought in for a kiss. The reader *needs* to see what that union would look like. If the chemistry described in the book blurb is really there."

"Chemistry?" *There's no chemistry between us,* Poppy wanted to argue. She glanced between the faces of the other women who were looking on. They were rapt and waiting.

There's no chemistry between us, right?

"I don't mind if you don't mind." William's voice was a low rumble. Poppy looked back at him sharply. By giving his consent to continue, he had highlighted her own uncertainty to the crowded room.

"I don't mind at all," she said. "Kiss me all you want."

"All right. I will."

Another long minute passed between them. Then the hand on her scalp tightened in resolution, and William leaned in. Poppy's heart raced as he placed a quick peck on her lips and withdrew. Disappointment flooded her, much more bitter than the adrenaline she had been feeling seconds earlier.

"Oh *nooo.* Not like that. You can't kiss her like that!" one of the authors moaned.

"We can't get a good photo unless you let it linger," another griped.

"After all that build-up, you can't just peck at her like a chicken!"

Poppy covered her mouth with her hand to hide her smile as William's eyes narrowed. "It helps if you remember that they're writers," she whispered between her fingers.

William's scowl deepened. "How could I forget?"

"They like deploying metaphors. Don't take it personally."

"She's a breathtakingly beautiful woman!" one of the other

authors called. "How can you look at her and be satisfied with something that…uninspired?"

"I never said anything about being satisfied," William growled below his breath. Their bodies were pressed so closely together that Poppy could feel his voice reverberating in his chest through her own. "I find this whole exercise unsatisfactory. And ridiculous."

"Shhh," Poppy hissed. The women were absorbed in their work, and she didn't want William's crankiness to throw cold water on the creative process. Then again, cold water might not be a bad idea. Her skin felt fever-hot. It must have only been her imagination; she was certain William was the kind of man to keep the temperature in his office strictly regulated. "What is this ridiculous desk for, if not to kiss a woman up against? Just pretend I'm someone you like if it makes it easier for you."

He studied her. They were so close she could see his eyes weren't as impenetrable as she had first imagined; in fact, they weren't even brown, but a dark meridian blue.

"I've never enjoyed taking what was easy," William murmured. His face leaned in toward her, and…

Poppy burst out laughing. It was a nervous giggle, and she was mortified in the aftermath—she hadn't interrupted a kiss like that since high school—but it was enough to halt the proceedings yet again. William's expression froze. His eyes caught fire, and the arms around her constricted like hot bands. Poppy opened her mouth to offer up an apology.

But suddenly there was no more room in her mouth for an apology, or words—there was barely enough room for her own tongue and teeth as William swooped in and captured her lips in a devastating kiss. Poppy had experienced only the barest taste of him before when he had kissed her, efficiently and stiffly, aware all the while of their audience; now, she was subsumed by him. He kissed her hard enough to force the small of her back up against his desk, but Poppy ignored the bite of the beast beneath her. They were both being conquered in that moment. Her hand came up to grip the back of William's neck as he pressed in, and her feet came up off the floor. He moved between her legs and pinned her against the desk. She couldn't break away if she wanted to, and boy, did she *not* want to. Escaping from William Jameson was the furthest thing from her mind. His mouth possessed the whole of her attention; his tongue swept the seam of her lips; his insistence could not be ignored…

Was she imagining things, or was the kiss accompanied by cheering and applause?

When William pulled away, he wore a look of triumph on his face. Poppy, delightfully dazed beneath him, noticed the light flush in his cheeks and disheveled hair. Maybe his victory wasn't as complete as he would like to think.

The authors hooted and hollered. This time, Poppy didn't apologize for her sheepish laugh. She tucked a stray strand of hair back behind her ear and allowed William to help her to her feet. "See? That wasn't so bad." She wished she didn't sound so out of breath.

"Not bad at all," William agreed. His hands lingered on her waist, and Poppy decided not to call attention to them. The authors descended, chattering excitedly; the whole meeting had been unorthodox from start to finish, but there was no lack of inspiration and activity in the room. It was exactly the sort of atmosphere Poppy had hoped to instigate, but she hadn't expected it to come at the price of a kiss. She sensed William's eyes on her; when she glanced up, he looked away, his attention conveniently called to one of the enthusiastic writers on his left. Poppy smiled to herself and stroked a hand along the glossy wood surface beneath her.

Maybe she could learn to love this damn desk, after all.

CHAPTER FIVE

WILLIAM

"Poppy."

The authors were all packing up to leave. Poppy was at the doorway to his office already. She turned when he called her back. Her long blonde hair, styled in ringlets for the meeting, swished and cascaded over her shoulder.

Was every move she made planned to perfection? Or was it possible that she was naturally, quite unassumingly, the most sexually appealing woman he had ever met?

Today had been a wake-up call. He vowed to set aside more time to think about the matter. Hell, it was probably asking too much of himself that he find time to schedule it. Poppy Hanniford wasn't someone to be scheduled. She was an invasive thought as much as she was a formidable rival, and William couldn't get enough of her. The challenge she posed was too addictive, and thinking about her…

Scratch thinking about her. *Not* thinking about her was becoming impossible.

"Can I speak to you in the hallway for a moment?" he asked her.

"Certainly, William."

He didn't allow his face to register surprise at also being called by his first name. He had just had Poppy Hanniford pinned beneath him on his desk; he had just had her pillowy lips crushed beneath his own. Their working relationship had changed in an instant, and they had shared that tectonic shift with an eager audience. It seemed ridiculous to keep sticking to the same old formalities now.

William walked with her toward the elevators. He had nothing left on his schedule for the day, but he always managed to find one project or another that required his intervention. He would get back to regular business as soon as he had seen her out.

"After your inspired little twist on the meeting in there, I've had some inspiration of my own," he admitted.

Poppy blinked in surprise. For a moment, those green eyes were completely unguarded, and William realized the implication of what he had just said. His quiet tone was undeniable; it sounded as if he was leading into asking her on a date.

"Really?" she replied. "I'd love to hear what you were thinking."

I'm not so certain you would. His thoughts when he had her up against the desk had been completely filthy. They were inescapable, and what's more, William didn't *want* to escape them. He wanted to vividly entertain every detail of what he would have done to her in such a compromising position had they not been sharing the room with seven others.

William punched the button for the ground floor and held the door for her—unnecessarily, but Poppy walked graciously beneath his arm. He followed closely behind.

"There is a new high ropes course that has gone up just outside of the city," he said. "Every major corporation has been hit with an invitation to host their team-building exercises there."

"I wouldn't know anything about being a major corporation." Poppy's lips quirked in that irresistibly knowing little smile of hers, and it was all William could do to leash himself from leaning in and tasting it. The doors of the elevator closed behind them, which made his impulse all the worse. He had never been around someone who tempted him to lose control like this before. It was intoxicating.

"Give yourself a bit more credit. Or don't," he added as an afterthought, "if that's part of what contributes to you getting ahead."

"I'm not being modest, William. I'm being objective. Wild-flower Agency is still a small fish compared to the shark that is Jameson Ad Agency. That being said, we did receive an invitation to try out the ropes course."

William snorted in amusement. "Finally, she gets back to the point."

"I promise you I never left."

"I'm proposing that we take advantage of the discount the course is offering at the moment. I need to refocus my team. I think it would benefit our work with the publishing house if we did it together."

"I disagree," Poppy said. "I've already checked out the ropes course online. I don't approve of the techniques they use. So much emphasis on physical strength and skill makes the course less accessible to the members of my team who aren't athletic. It would only promote disunity, if you ask me. And I think we can both agree that's not the best way to go about building up team morale."

"An interesting point," William noted. The elevator ground to a halt, and the doors folded open. "…but then again, it could also be that you simply aren't up to the challenge of leading your team through the exercises."

His words seemed to echo through the empty lobby. Neither of them moved. The doors held a moment longer, then closed over them again.

"Frankly, William, my team would kick your team's collective ass," she said. "If you think I'm afraid of a challenge, then I'm afraid you don't know the first thing about me."

"Oh, I think I know one or two things about you," he murmured. He canted his shoulder toward her, but kept his hands in his pockets. He didn't want to remind her just *what* he had learned about her up there in his office.

"I never expected you to resort to schoolyard tactics," she said. "This is the equivalent of calling me out for being a chicken."

"You can look at it as a double dog dare, if you prefer."

Poppy laughed. "All right, William. I'll take you up on your offer... even if I think there are better options out there."

"Not offer," he corrected mildly. "Challenge. I'll even make a bet with you: the first person to get their team through the ropes course gets to take the lead on the convention project."

Poppy turned and held her hand out to him. "You were right after all. You do know a thing or two about me. You know how to phrase a challenge in a way I can't resist. It's a deal."

The door opened on their handshake. William remained in the elevator, watching her take the long walk down the lobby and out the revolving glass door. She never looked back over her shoulder, but something in him knew that *she* knew that he was watching.

She wasn't the only one who had trouble resisting a challenge.

"Hang Ten" was not the most inspired of company names. Seeing it emblazoned on the envelope of his invitation had almost been enough cause to throw it in the garbage, but William was glad now that he hadn't completely discounted the offer.

The ropes course was gorgeous: the minds behind it had spared no expense. Every penny they had pinched when it came to testing their brand name had apparently been put to use erecting structures that rose forty, maybe even fifty feet off the ground. There was also a deep, man-made "canyon" further up the way that William had immediately taken note of while browsing the website. It was advertised enticingly as being "for experienced climbers only".

William was no stranger to heights: he enjoyed rock climbing, and made it to the gym near his office at least three times a week. He wanted a piece of that canyon.

But it wasn't the only thing he wanted a piece of.

He hadn't had a chance to speak to Poppy yet. Not that he should be seeking out his competition other than to intimidate, but William had been counting on some good old-fashioned trash talk—and more than a little bit of flirting—and he hadn't gotten anywhere near his quota yet.

He moved off from where his team was and approached Poppy. His eyes roamed her skin-tight climbing gear appreciatively. Her body looked so much more athletic, so much more sleek and streamlined, than he had expected. This might prove a challenge after all. She was currently directing a young man with black hair to tie the knots of everyone on the team. William watched the boy struggle, raising an eyebrow of disbelief, but his attention was quickly diverted elsewhere.

"Good afternoon, William." Poppy didn't so much as glance up from her supervision. "Looks like my team got here first. How about we sweeten our team wager with an individual bet?" She beat him to the first word of greeting and launched them immediately ahead in the conversation. It impressed and amused him in equal turns. William glanced behind him, and saw that various members of his own team were standing close enough to hear the exchange. Poppy had to be aware of their audience.

"I was just about to propose something similar," he said. "What terms?"

"First one of us to reach the bottom of the canyon can blend members of both our teams for the convention tasks," Poppy said immediately. She turned away from her assistant and straightened. The front of her athletic top was unzipped far enough that William could see the top of her sports bra. By any account, it shouldn't have been as provocative as it was…but all he could think about in that moment was what her body had felt like beneath his own, trapped against his desk. He had replayed the memory of their kiss over and over and over again. He had started to imagine what would have happened had there not been an audience there in the room with them.

"Deal," he said. Poppy nodded and grinned at his agreement. She offered her hand, and William shook it. He let their clasped palms linger, and Poppy didn't disappoint; she held him just as hard. Their union was only interrupted when the instructor cleared his throat.

"So, you two want the advanced course first?" he asked hesitantly.

"Yes," they both said as one. Their eyes remained focused on each other.

"Okay. Right. Well, follow me, then…"

The instructor called for several golf carts to be brought around, and the teams were ferried out to the edge of the property. William pulled his harness on as he stepped to the canyon crevice and looked over. It was a long, sheer drop. The rappel would be difficult, especially for someone who had never attempted anything like this before. He glanced toward Poppy out of the corner of his eye, but if the woman was afraid of the task she had set for them both, she didn't show it. She spoke with the instructor as he helped her into her own harness. William watched the placement of the other man's hands carefully, and felt a surge of something he hadn't felt in a long time: jealousy. It was sharp and bitter and strangely invigorating. It was a call to action, a call to compete.

He approached them in a moment, letting his own hand fall to the small of her back as he steered her toward the ledge. Poppy didn't shake him off her, even though they were meant to be keeping up appearances for the sake of their teams. He withdrew the hand before his touch could translate as suspicious. He dangled himself over the cliff side, feet braced, hanging onto his tether with two clenched hands.

"Ready?" he called over to her.

"Ready." She positioned herself similarly beside him.

"Begin!" their instructor called.

And they were off. William let the rope slide between his fingers effortlessly as he gave his body over to space. Exhilaration raced through him as he dropped. He glanced over, and was surprised to see Poppy dropping at the same speed, if not faster. He watched her form with approval—it took guts to rappel that fast, especially considering her lack of experience. He increased his own speed. He was determined not to lose.

"How are you holding up, Wildflower?" he called over breathlessly after a few minutes. The rush of wind past his face and down his neck was unlike anything he experienced at the gym. He really needed to get out and do this more often…

Poppy was silent on his right. William glanced her way, curious. He was about to overtake her, but she didn't appear to be actively descending anymore. Her eyes were fixed on something just above her.

"William…" There was panic in her voice. William's eyes snapped to the source of her attention. The knot above her was unraveling. The rope slithered in on itself like the coils of a snake. It would release her in the next moment

He reacted instantaneously. He shoved off with his boot and flew to her. He slung an arm around her waist, and Poppy's own arms came up; she gave a half-strangled cry of fear as the rope unraveled, but he was there, and he wasn't going to let her fall. She held onto him as he executed a quick series of maneuvers that ended in him clamping her harness to his with a spare carabiner. He glanced up, but they were too far down for him to see what the reaction was on the faces above.

"Going down!" he shouted up to the instructor. He didn't wait for a response; he assumed immediate charge of the situation. He needed to get them safely to the ground, *now*. They descended together, Poppy secured to his side, her arms wrapped around his neck. He didn't stop until they reached the ground, and he was forced to do so out of necessity; only then did he allow his grip on her waist to loosen. After a moment, Poppy unwound her arms from around him.

"Are you all right?" He stroked a stray piece of her hair aside. Her hands settled against his chest. She was breathing hard; if he took her in his arms now, he thought he would feel her racing heart for himself. He was sorely tempted to do just that, but he knew they were being watched above.

"Yes," Poppy replied finally, shakily. "I think you just saved my life, William."

"Don't think any more about it," he replied. He hadn't for a second questioned what he would have to do to ensure her safety, and he didn't think he deserved any gratitude. Still, if his split-second decision was the reason Poppy stayed so close to him now, he wouldn't try too hard to talk her out of her feelings. She stepped back finally, away from him, and William gave her a moment to compose herself. She unclipped her harness and let it drop; before it hit the ground, she caught the frayed rope and held it. Her expression was an impenetrable mask. She let it slip from her fingers eventually as William shimmied out of his own equipment.

"I'm all right! We're all right!" she called up to her team. She waved, and several figures waved back. At least, William thought they did, but they were so far overhead it was hard to be sure.

"Looks like we're stuck down here for a bit," he said.

"Alone," Poppy added.

Together, he thought. But he didn't say it.

The word hung in the air between them as loudly as if he had.

෴

"William…" Poppy began.

William knew what was coming. But he let her say it anyway.

"I am *so* sorry," she said. "This is all my fault."

"Not all your fault," William allowed. They sat together against the base of the wall. He would never admit it out loud to his fiercest competitor, but he needed a moment to regain his breath—not because the climb down had been arduous, but because his heart still raced with the memory of seeing Poppy in trouble. If he had frozen, even for a second, to debate the logistics of what he needed to do, she would have unraveled and fallen out of reach. He wasn't used to letting outside forces get the better of him, not even gravity.

Only Poppy had ever really challenged his authority and won.

"It *might* all be my fault," she pressed. She watched him as he pulled out his cell phone to text for a car to come get them. "I…so there's this intern. He's…"

"Dyed black hair, illogical haircut, piercings inappropriate for any workplace?" William stared hard at her, and Poppy ducked her head and blushed. He reached out to push the curtain of her blonde hair aside. She was the last woman he would allow to hide herself from him. "I remember. You had a name for him."

"His name is Duncan. We usually just call him Emo Kid." Poppy sighed. "I think he prefers his nickname, actually. Well, I would if I *believed* he had many preferences outside of the ones he harbors for disruptive music and the color black."

"What does an intern have to do with any of this?" William

asked. "Not that I don't expect you to take full responsibility for the shortcomings of your team members."

"Thanks for that!" Poppy winced a smile. William realized his hand remained beside her ear, caressing her temple, but she didn't comment on it. He drew it away only when she continued speaking, hoping she wouldn't have noticed the lingering touch...almost ready to dare her to mention it. Maybe it was the adrenaline still coursing through his veins that made him feel so reckless. "That's what I'm trying to do, though. Take responsibility. I let Emo Kid tie the knot. I thought it would inspire him to focus."

Poppy sighed again and dropped her head back against the wall, letting her wrists dangle loosely on her knees. William watched her every move, still assessing her for any sign of injury, but his mind raced to process what she was saying. "You need to fire the kid," he said pointblank. "His oversight was inexcusable. I have a feeling it's always been, and you've just been too nice to say anything."

"I'm not too nice!" Poppy fired back. "I'm just not totally ruthless like the rest of you macho ad execs. And you *are* all men, need I remind you. Just because I prefer to fill a supportive role doesn't make me a doormat."

"If you say so," he replied. He wasn't convinced.

Poppy shook her head. "You don't understand. *Not* acting supportive is what got us into this mess today. I like to promote the best in everyone, and I don't normally hesitate to act when the best idea is presented to me." She surprised him by reaching between them to pick his hand up out of the dirt. "But I let the spirit of our competition get the best of me," she admitted. "I've never gone head-to-head with someone so…well, like I was saying. I let my feelings get the better of me. I haven't been myself since this whole thing started."

Neither have I, William wanted to say. *Despite my best efforts. And despite what you think.*

"What are you saying?" he asked instead. He could feel this was leading up to something.

"I'm saying that I want *you* to take the lead at the convention, William," Poppy concluded. "Wildflower Agency isn't backing out, but I'm stepping back from our own little competition. I think you're the best person to take charge. I can do better promoting and supporting the group from within. I think this arrangement is the best thing for everyone involved."

William's head spun. Despite Poppy's insistence that he take charge, she had arrived at her decision in record time…and she certainly hadn't run her decision by *him.*

His phone buzzed, indicating a text from their driver. The car was on its way. William pocketed his phone, thinking that he would hold off on relaying this information until he could convince Poppy to reconsider, but she was already forging ahead.

"… so anyway, now that that's settled, I was thinking we should go as a couple to the convention," she said. "I mean, not a *couple*-couple, but a famous literary couple. Tons of people will be cosplaying, and we can use the opportunity to illustrate the concept of our panel. You know what I mean. Anyway, I was thinking maybe Bella and Edward, at least for the first day?"

"God no." The refusal was out of his mouth before he could

think how to steer their conversation back on track. Her suggestion evoked an image of himself, pale and glittering, dressed like an undead high schooler...such a vision must be nipped in the bud. "*That* couples' costume idea was beaten to death already ten years ago."

"Pun intended?" Poppy's mouth quirked, but he was on a roll and couldn't be distracted.

"Even taking the wearisome history into consideration, with the amount of Edwards and Bellas we're bound to see at the convention...we'd get lost in the crowd. We'd be totally unremarkable, when the theme of our panel is *unconventional*. And anyway, we look nothing like the characters."

"How about Jamie and Claire? Outlander?" she suggested.

William gave a disgusted snort. "At least Edward and Bella were subtextually abusive and unhealthy. Can you imagine the number of convention-goers to come up and ask us if we'd ever recreated that scene where..." He stopped. Poppy was gazing up at him, eyes shining, her voluptuous mouth even fuller than usual and unable to contain a smile of absolute amusement.

"You've read all these books," she said triumphantly. "You're a romance-lover. This convention was *made* for people like you."

"I..." There was no use denying it by this point. William didn't know what part of his reputation was still salvageable, but he decided to take a leaf out of Poppy's book and charge ahead. "You didn't trick me into admitting anything, Miss Hanniford. It's certainly not a secret to those who know me best."

"Romance-lover!" she said again gleefully. She rocked back with the force of her laugh, her shoulder brushing against his own. "No wonder you want their business so badly! Do you think they'll send you free books? Oh, I'd hate to be the one to take that *hookup* away from you…"

A fire flared in William. "You won't be taking any 'hookups' away from me," he promised. "In fact—"

When Poppy's lips closed momentarily over her smile, likely to say something else to try and get a rise out of him, William made his move. He caught her chin and swooped in, capturing her lips with his own. The kiss was firm, authoritative, *deliberate*. As sensual as it was silencing. He held it for longer than he had intended, enjoying her surprised intake of breath and denying her real release until he was satisfied. He withdrew slowly, enjoying the way her plump bottom lip tasted, and the way it fell back into place once he had finished his surprise sampling. Gorgeous green eyes gazed at him; for once, William couldn't read a single secret thought hidden in their depths. Poppy broadcasted everything she was thinking on her face in that moment.

He found the sight immensely satisfying.

"William…" Almost as satisfying as the way she breathed his name. "You should know I'm thinking about backing away from this contract. It's getting too complicated. Things between us…" She trailed off.

"Poppy. I don't want to end our competition," he whispered. He stroked her cheek, marveling at how her skin seemed to glow in the fading light from the sun. "And neither do you. Besides, it wouldn't be half as fun without you."

Poppy's lips parted. Maybe she meant to respond, or maybe she meant to follow-up some other way. William leaned in.

The pop of gravel beneath car tires pulled him back to the present. Poppy moved her head away to look, and William followed her gaze. The car was coming down the road to retrieve them. He mentally cursed the fact that he had texted them so soon to begin with. He rose, and offered his hand to Poppy, who didn't hesitate in letting him pull her to her feet. He gathered their equipment as she conversed with the driver. *Probably to thank him,* William thought. Poppy never let any small job or gesture go unnoticed.

"I meant what I said," she told William as he held the car door open for her. "I'd like the best person to win the job, William. And if today's… conversation… proved anything to me, it's that you're a good fit. I'm not beyond admitting when I'm defeated."

"We'll see," he allowed as he got in beside her. He had already decided privately that he wasn't going to let Poppy Hanniford slip out of this arrangement so easily. He wasn't going to accept any sort of victory that wasn't hard-won… and he *definitely* wasn't going to accept her easy exit from his life. Not now that he had tasted her lips. Not now that she had become so thoroughly entangled in his thoughts.

There was no way he was going to let her call the shots. He was going to have his way, and he was going to prove that his methods were the right way to win.

He would get what he wanted.

CHAPTER SIX

POPPY

"I swear," Poppy said. "Isn't it weird for you sometimes? I mean, if you really sit back and allow yourself to think about it?"

"Think about what?" Across the table from her, William was busy pulling his tablet out of his briefcase. "I try to have a plan for every scenario, if you haven't noticed."

Poppy arched an eyebrow. "I've noticed," she returned coolly. The two of them were seated at a coffee shop a few blocks east from Wildflower Agency headquarters...and a few blocks west of Jameson headquarters. It felt almost Shakespearean: 'two lovers from rival clans sneak out to a hideaway between their strongholds'. Or something like that. Poppy hadn't exactly excelled in classic literature in school. She had always found the majority of it as dry and dusty as the history it hailed from.

No, what she loved most was romance: timeless, sweeping.

Forbidden.

"So am I supposed to assume it was your plan all along that *we* would collaborate together on…on…" Poppy gestured to the stack of folders between them. "On Conventional Romance?"

"I assure you, Miss Hanniford, I find nothing about our present partnership conventional," William said as he reached for his coffee.

Poppy's cheeks heated. "You can say that again," she muttered. It was the perfect segue into a topic that had been nagging her. There was no good time to bring it up, really, but she still felt as if she needed to clear the air. "William, I want you to know that I—that this interpersonal *thing* going on between us isn't something I normally encourage."

"Nor I." William squinted at his tablet screen. It was a look of doomed concentration, one that clearly asked: *how is everyone else getting on? Why can't I connect to the Wi-Fi?*

"William!" Poppy reached over and wrenched the tablet out of his hands. William stared at his empty palms as if he couldn't believe she had just snatched it away. He had been born filthy rich, after all: he had probably never experienced someone taking a toy away from him in his life. "William, I mean it. What I'm trying to say is…" Poppy closed her eyes as she fought for the right words. "…I don't normally do this sort of thing. Like, ever. That came out way more anticlimactic than I wanted, but I hope you know what I mean. I don't normally kiss rival CEOs, especially not those I'm competing against for a job."

"I know what you mean." William met her eyes patiently.

"And I mean it when I say that the same goes for me. But you don't believe me, do you?"

"Not for a second." William was *way* too handsome to have avoided this sort of entanglement in the past. The odds simply weren't in his favor.

"Well, I've never found myself in a working partnership with a rival CEO before," William said as he took his tablet back from her. "So whether or not you believe me is irrelevant. You're the only one, Poppy. I'm as new to this sort of thing as you are."

"Surely you aren't *totally* new?" Poppy said with a raised eyebrow. William rolled his eyes at the low-hanging fruit, and she stifled a laugh. She had never seen William Jameson roll his eyes before. It must be something he reserved for private moments, she realized, when the eyes of the world were finally off him. She wondered what it meant that he would do it in front of her.

"William…there's something else," she began hesitantly. She had intended to use their meeting today to tell him of her decision to forfeit the job. It was painful to admit it, but Jameson Ad Agency was a better fit for this client. After seeing William in action last weekend, Poppy felt certain of it. The only thing hampering the project going forward was her own team's involvement. Sooner or later, there would be too many people running in too many different directions, and their productivity would tank. Better to back out now, gracefully, and let William…

"… so you understand the conundrum I'm facing, and I'm hoping you can assist me on this," William was saying. Poppy blinked and glanced up. She had been shredding her napkin into little pieces and not listening, but that didn't mean she couldn't set her own agenda aside and rise to the occasion.

"I'd be happy to, William! Only there's just a *small* caveat: I didn't go to school to be a Jameson's assistant," Poppy said innocently. "Are you sure I'm qualified for the position?"

"Oh, knock it off." William flipped his tablet around and passed it back to her. "Look. The publishing house has just announced what the basis for the convention is going to be this year. They've already selected the book."

"Gone with the Wind!" Poppy exclaimed. Her heart leapt at the sight of the familiar movie poster: Scarlett O'Hara and Rhett Butler, locked in their iconic embrace amid the bright orange fire engulfing the Old South.

William leaned forward. "You know it?"

"Of *course* I know it! What heartless, cultureless bridge troll hasn't seen Gone with…the…oh," Poppy concluded at William's look. "Well, if it makes you feel any better, I never did get all the way through the book."

"I didn't even know it was a book first," William said blandly. He sat back in his chair and looked thoughtful.

"But I do love the movie. It's one of my all-time favorites," she volunteered. "Well, I don't love the racial slurs. Or *other* problematic elements."

"Glad to hear it, Poppy." William chuckled. "At least that's one aspect of the story we can agree not to include in our planning for the event."

His emphasis on the word 'our' was enough to make her sit up and take notice. She watched William take a casual sip of his coffee. Evidently he hadn't noticed his own usage of the word. Was he really ready to play ball as part of a team?

Poppy squinted at him. He looked the same as ever: regal, collected, and completely absorbed in the task before him. She couldn't count on seeing a change of heart in William Jameson this early in their collaboration, no matter how much she might like to fantasize about him being a team player. She was sure *that* would come with time, especially after he got a taste of how easy she was to work with…

But in the meantime, he would never know how effective a team could really be if she backed out now. Poppy doubted anyone in his own agency had the balls to suggest as much to their CEO, much less follow through. More than that, maybe she had the publishing house all wrong. Poppy could admit when she was wrong—especially when her misunderstanding had blinded her to her own advantage. If the convention was using *Gone with the Wind* as its theme, then the event was obviously seeking to prop up strong women. Poppy had always likened herself to Scarlett O'Hara growing up—to the admirable, tenacious aspects, anyway—and the fact that her potential client had chosen that particular story had to be a sign. They were trying to prop up narratives with strong female characters, strong *women,* and Poppy had always counted herself among them. She couldn't erase herself from the narrative before it had even really begun.

She couldn't back down and let William take over now.

"What are you smiling about?" William sounded playfully suspicious, but Poppy could hear the smile in his own voice. She shook her head, grinning, and stabbed at her pastry with her fork. "Poppy…"

"What? Nothing! I'm smiling at nothing! I mean, even if I was smiling…" Her grin broadened. "Can't I enjoy a morning out with my rival?"

"I'm enjoying myself too," William acknowledged.

"Enjoying yourself with your tablet!" she teased.

"I'm sorry if I get wrapped up in work." He surprised her by setting the tablet aside and folding his hands. "The best defense I can offer you is that it's my personality type. Always has been. But…it's remarkable to have someone to bounce ideas off of, and get lost in a problem with company."

Poppy shook her head again. "Honestly, William, I'm just giving you a hard time. I really admire your concentration, your dedication. No wonder you're so successful."

"I'm starting to think that success comes with a cost," William murmured. He spoke so quietly that Poppy almost imagined she had misheard him. She blinked, and leaned in a little in case he decided to follow up his words, but he seemed to be talking more to himself than to his tablemate.

"Maybe it doesn't have to." Poppy reached across the table and pulled one of his hands free to hold in hers. She lost herself momentarily in the feeling of his long strong fingers, and the deep crease of his palm. His hand was still warm from the mug of coffee.

"Miss Hanniford. You'll set the gossip columns talking," William whispered, but he didn't pull away. His serious mouth curled in a crooked, mischievous smile, and only one dimple leapt into prominence. Poppy had never seen him wear that version of his smile before. She wondered what a man who smiled like that was secretly capable of, and a rush of warmth flooded through her. Her face suddenly felt hot, hotter than their joined hands. The place between her crossed legs doubly so.

"Do you care?" She was genuinely curious.

William seemed to consider for a moment. His fingers caressed the inside of hers all the while. "I don't," he said finally. "Not in the least. My younger brother has occupied those particular New York columns long enough. Maybe he's overdue for a challenger to his crown."

"Then you'll wear all the crowns in the family," Poppy laughed.

"Are you calling me a king, Miss Hanniford?"

"Like you've never heard that comparison before." Poppy withdrew her hand from William's and rose. She hated that she was the first to notice the time, but he was sitting just below the coffee shop's clock. She enjoyed the momentary look of confusion that passed across his face, and filed it away as a victory.

William Jameson had been so wrapped up in her that he had forgotten the time.

"I propose we meet again at the end of the week," she said as they shouldered their bags and walked out together. "But I get to decide the time and place."

"Done," William said. "I think a follow-up meeting is a good idea. I'll try not to be so distracted next time."

"See that you aren't." Poppy paused on the sidewalk outside and smiled up at him. "Because the meeting I'm proposing could be *rife* with distractions. I'm inviting you over to watch 'Gone with the Wind', William. Friday night, eight o'clock, my place. Can't serve a client when you're totally ignorant of what they're looking for, can you?"

"I wouldn't say I'm *totally* ignorant," William fired back. "Eight o'clock. Text me the address."

Poppy waved and turned. She was surprised when William caught the strap of her messenger bag and reeled her back suddenly. She turned herself around just in time to crash against his chest. She gazed up the length of his expensive tie, totally stricken by the move and trying to hide the fact. He looked down at her, his dark eyes penetrating. For a moment, Poppy thought he was going to capture her mouth in a kiss right then and there, in full view of the interested coffee shop patrons. But William didn't budge, and neither did she. If this was a test, she was determined to pass it. She wouldn't be the first to admit defeat in this particular little battle.

Even if the lips hovering above her looked absolutely irresistible.

"Don't be late," she breathed.

"I wouldn't dream of it," William replied. The arm around her waist relented, and she slipped free of him once more. She took a step back, then turned away again. She tried not to notice the collective look of disappointment on the faces of the coffee shop watchers as she strolled back down the street toward her office. She tried to ignore the way her heart kept beating, fast and irregular, all throughout her morning appointments. She swore it didn't calm down until lunchtime, and a text from William requesting her address started it going all over again.

Maybe it was all the coffee.

Maybe she wasn't as resilient as she thought.

CHAPTER SEVEN

WILLIAM

William arrived early and took a moment to himself on the stoop of Poppy's brownstone to adjust his tie. He had already checked his appearance in the tinted window of his limousine and knew he looked as put-together as always.

He just didn't feel that way. The prospect of seeing Poppy Hanniford tended to do that to him.

The handle of his briefcase was worn and smooth and reassuring in his hand. He had no idea what he was about to walk into, but he had come prepared. He wouldn't put it past Poppy to try and throw him a curveball the moment she opened her door to him. He raised his fist and knocked.

The door opened. Poppy stood before him, grinning. "You came!" she exclaimed, as if there had ever been any question. She held a massive bowl of popcorn in her arms, salted and glistening and ready for consumption. The bowl was almost wider around than her arms could reach.

William's gaze went lower and lower, trying to wrap his head around what he was seeing. Poppy stood before him in an over-sized T-shirt (purple, of course) with large black print letters.

"What is 'Netflix and Chill'?" he read by way of greeting.

Poppy glanced down at her T-shirt logo. "You really don't know?" She grinned. "It's code," she said mysteriously.

"Whatever it is, it reads like it should have a hashtag in front of it."

"Perceptive," she commended him. "Let's just say it's some-thing those whippersnappers on the Internet cooked up. I figured it was probably lame enough by now for someone my age to ironically appropriate it."

"Looks like I came overdressed for the occasion," William remarked.

"For movie night? Yeah, I'd say so." Poppy laughed disarm-ingly as he followed her inside. "You came dressed just fine, William. Actually, I've imagined that you sleep in your suits. So thanks for adding fuel to my theory."

"That would be my brother, Sam," William said without missing a beat. "Although I appreciate that you imagine me sleeping."

Poppy's cheeks colored a little, but she didn't look shy or sheepish. If there was anything William had come to understand about her, it was that she enjoyed his flirtation as much as he did —and gave as good as she got. "Here," she said. She plucked a kernel of popcorn off the top of the bowl. "Open up and tell me if it's good."

William set his briefcase aside on her kitchen table, and

opened his mouth obediently. She popped the fluffy piece in, and he closed his lips over it, purposefully catching her finger in the process. She withdrew her hand and pretended not to notice. "It's good. Tasty," he said. "Reminds me of how my mother used to make it."

"I take that as a very high compliment," Poppy said. "Shall we?"

His days of opposition research into Poppy Hanniford were over...or at least, postponed until an indefinite future date, but that didn't prevent William from taking in every inch of her apartment now. She led him into the den—accented in a deep, luxurious purple, of course. She made what William had once thought a garish color appear like a beautiful shade newly discovered on the spectrum. Every table, every surface, in every room, seemed to have a potted plant growing on it, and they looked better watered and better looked-after then even the ones back at the office, and William hired a guy to take care of that. Poppy's brownstone was tasteful, well-kept, and homey. William felt a strange sensation forming within him. It wasn't nostalgia, and it wasn't longing...it was something else, some indefinable cousin of the two. In Poppy's apartment, he felt it for the first time.

"Thanks for agreeing to host," he said as he collapsed back into her couch. The cushions sagged beneath him, almost threatening to engulf him entirely. He had never been so goddamn comfortable in his life.

Poppy alighted on the cushion beside him. "Not at all. It's the least I can do, considering it's one of my favorite movies."

"You keep saying that," William mused as she booted up the DVD player. "I wonder if I stand to learn something new about you before this night is through. Something intimate."

"Did I mention the movie is four hours long?" Poppy said perkily.

William groaned. He rose to go get his laptop from the kitchen to take notes. When he returned, Poppy was reclined back next to the indent he had left. Her eyes narrowed at the laptop, but she said nothing. She didn't have to—it was obvious she disapproved.

William took steadfast notes for the first twenty minutes of the movie...but soon enough he found his keystrokes slowing, his eyes favoring one screen more than the other. He had thought watching a four-hour plot unfold would be tedious, but he found himself totally engrossed in Scarlett's plight. He closed his laptop, set it aside, and relaxed back. He was surprised to find his shoulder resting against Poppy's.

"Welcome to the movie," she said with a teasing grin. "Popcorn? Or are you going to make me eat it all myself?"

Two hours in, and the bowl was empty. William leaned forward, squinting at the drama playing out on the TV screen. "You know, I never realized this movie had such a strong female character," he said. "For its time, and even for now." He didn't mention aloud that he thought he could relate to Scarlett. Poppy disappeared into the kitchen, and returned with two freshly-cracked, frosted beers. She offered one to William, and he accepted without hesitation. She sat back down.

"You're kidding, right?" Poppy took a long swig of her beer.

"I mean, *yes* she's unbelievably strong and cool... but she's an amazing character because she's flawed. They all are. In Scarlett's case," Poppy gestured toward the screen with the butt of her bottle, "her stubbornness is her downfall. She should rely on Rhett more when he offers her his help. She should trust his love for her."

"From where I'm sitting, Scarlett's doing exactly what she needs to keep her family and her plantation afloat," William said. "She's a passionate woman, but she's also making calculated decisions about survival. Decisions that aren't easy for anyone. Depending on somebody else..." William shook his head and chuckled. "That wouldn't make her such a remarkable leading woman. You can't be a leading woman if you don't *lead.*"

Poppy shrugged. "We'll see," she said.

William didn't like the promise in her voice. He liked it even less when, two hours later, the movie ended, and the unspoken promise was fulfilled: Scarlett was left alone.

William stared at the blank television screen long after the movie had concluded. Then he turned to Poppy.

"Well?" Her jade green eyes shone within the darkness. "Did you totally love it? I bet you have some criticisms. Of *course* you have criticisms."

"It isn't a perfect love story," William said. "That much is obvious. With how hard Scarlett worked...there was no real emotional payoff for either her or the audience in the end. Her family, and Rhett—absolutely none of them showed appreciation for how much she toiled and sacrificed. Scarlett single-handedly improved the course of her life and the lives of those around her, and this is how the narrative thanks her?"

"Wow." Poppy stared at him, before taking a quick swig of her third beer…at least, William thought it was her third. "You really took this movie to heart."

"I wouldn't take it otherwise," he said. "You said it's one of your favorite love stories."

"My single favorite love story, actually."

"I just don't understand it," he muttered. His tongue felt loose, his wit completely agile. He wasn't so far gone as to *not* suspect the beer, but it was easier to go with the flow of his feelings.

"What don't you understand?"

"Why none of *them* understood!" William exclaimed. "I mean, it's obvious to the viewer that Scarlett got stuck with a shitty ending, isn't it?"

"Of course she did," Poppy said. "Because she was *flawed,* William. Her life's tragedy is realizing too late that what she wanted was standing right in front of her the whole time. Scarlett messed up by never inviting anyone else into her world—into her *plans.*"

"She doesn't want a man like Rhett anyway," William muttered as he sank back into the couch. "Seriously, what a clown. 'You should be kissed, and kissed often, and by someone who knows how.' *Christ.* Just shoot me if anything that cheesy ever comes out of my mouth."

"You're drunk," Poppy accused abruptly. She swayed a little herself as she pointed to him. "And also, you're *wrong*. That's one of the single most romantic things a man has said to a woman, *ever.* And you know what? I don't care if it *was* fictional!"

"And you stand by your claim?" William asked her.

"I stand by my claim." Poppy crossed her arms.

"Didn't look to me like he had the kissing chops to back up his offer," he countered. "If I was Rhett, I would have grabbed the woman I loved that instant, kissed her, and never let her go. I would have made her see just how much she needs me."

"No kiss is *that* good," Poppy argued. Then she snorted and set her beer aside. "I mean, come on...I can only suspend my disbelief so far. Even audiences back in the forties would have rolled their eyes if that was the case."

"Maybe," William acquiesced. "Maybe none of them ever experienced the kind of kiss I'm talking about."

Green eyes gleamed even brighter in the darkness. The low light cast by the television screen bathed Poppy in a soft, silver radiance. William hadn't allowed himself expectations for how this evening would go—not conscious ones, anyway—but he was feeling too good to stop now. The silence between them tasted of expectation.

Of challenge.

He grabbed a fistful of Poppy's shirt and pulled her over to his cushion. He swept his free hand down the curve of her cheek, watching her lean into the touch with a sigh, almost as if she had stopped thinking and was only responding to him now. *Good.* That was exactly how he wanted her. When her eyes fluttered open again, William moved in. He crushed his lips against hers in the dark. He didn't need a light to see by. If he didn't know where her mouth was, he knew *exactly* where it belonged, and that's what guided him to her. He tasted the spark of carbonation, the sweet, slick hint of butter on her lips lubricating his every plunge and slide. It was unlike any kiss they had shared before, and unlike anything William had experienced with a woman.

So he kept going.

"God," Poppy moaned when she was able to draw back minutes later. William lowered himself to sample the smooth skin of her throat; he enjoyed the way her words trembled as a result. "You have no idea how long I've waited...*waited* for a man to try and live up to that kiss..."

He intended to do more than just try. He silenced Poppy with another press of his lips to hers, and let his hand wander up her thigh to her hip. The denim cut-offs she wore were as short as her shirt was long. There was plenty of smooth skin for him to touch, but 'plenty' wasn't nearly enough.

William pushed her back into the couch as his fingers located the front of her shorts. Poppy undulated her hips to give him better access; her hands came up to cup his face, to pull him deeper into the kiss. It wasn't enough. He felt like he could never get enough of her, but he was sure as hell going to try.

The button on her shorts came undone, and he guided the cut-offs down her wiggling hips. He let the zipper on her fly come free on its own. Poppy arched beneath him, writhing and kicking her legs until her shorts went sailing off into a far corner of the room.

He couldn't get her out of that shirt fast enough. He would

never understand women's fascination with oversized clothes, although he supposed it was probably a relief to get into them after a long day at the office. Poppy's loud choice of shirt made his job easy now. He stripped it up over her head, exposing the black outline of the bra beneath. It was svelte and womanly by contrast, and obviously from a high-end store; it matched her black lace panties. *These* garments appeared to have been created with the exact opposite philosophy of whoever was responsible for that shirt. William silently thanked the manufacturer as he let his eyes travel over her.

"I'm pretty sure Rhett never looked at Scarlett like *that,*" Poppy murmured. "Mr. Jameson, what do you intend to do with me?" She reached for him, and William bent obediently. This time when their lips moved together, their tongues tangled. The kiss was indulgent, almost lazy. His hands slid between them to continue their work. He had no intention of spending all night admiring the way Poppy's underwear perfectly complemented her body. He was going to divest her of every inch of it, *now.*

"What I intend to do with you, Miss Hanniford, is confidential Jameson business," William whispered. Her hands were loosening his tie now and parting the collar of his shirt. "Though I suppose since it's been proven by now that we work so well together…"

"… you'd be willing to make a small concession for me?" Poppy asked, batting her eyes.

"For the particular collaboration I have in mind?" William thrust his straining erection against her to punctuate his point, and she gasped appreciatively. "Anything but small, Miss Hanniford."

Her hands worked even more quickly after that to strip his clothes off him. It was just as William feared—he was over-dressed—but Poppy's fingers were as dexterous as they were eager. He could easily imagine that she had mapped her route to getting him naked ahead of time. He had certainly done the same for her in every meeting they had ever shared. He let her strip his clothes off, one article at a time, as he drew his wallet out of his pocket and thumbed it open. There it was, the sleek black package from the box of Trojan Magnums he had purchased days ago after their charged kiss. He drew it out and tossed his wallet to the side carelessly.

He aligned his naked body with her own, privately enjoying the feel of skin-on-skin contact. Poppy hooked one leg around his waist to keep herself from sinking too far back into the cush-ions. Her body was perfect. Her *curves* were perfect. Her nipples were pointed, and hard with her need for him. She stared up at him with that angelic face of hers, pillowed in a cushion of golden hair, and William's cock twitched violently at the look in her eyes. He had never had a woman give him such pleasure with her eyes alone. She looked equal parts winded by him and hungry for him. It was an expression he would never allow himself to forget.

"Touch me," he whispered. Poppy complied. Her smooth, cool hands found him and clasped his shaft. She ran her fingers along the length of his cock, and William hissed. He strained at her touch. It was too teasing. He needed heat, pressure. He needed to know the most secret part of her. If he didn't fuck Poppy, *now,* he would explode. Every muscle in his body tensed in anticipation of the next moment.

"I want you," Poppy murmured. Her eyelids fell to half-mast, and fuck if William would ever forget that expression, either. "Please, William…"

No need for politeness. They were beyond that now. If William stopped to think, he would realize they were well beyond anything he had prepared for when he had entered into this tentative partnership—but there was no time to think. There was only Poppy, and *now.* There was only his hand gliding between her legs to test her readiness and coming away wet. There was only that little pearl, perfectly nestled above her entrance, and what he could do to her by pressing it.

"William!" Poppy said his name *very* differently this time. She gasped and bucked and surged beneath him as he rolled her clit, taking easy mastery of her pleasure. He experimented by applying different amounts of pressure, until a touch of his finger was enough to make her cry and clutch him so hard he nearly fell off the couch. Her hands clenched around his cock as she rolled the condom onto it, and William groaned. It still wasn't enough.

"Don't make me ask again," Poppy panted.

"I wouldn't dream of it, Miss Hanniford."

He hiked her other leg up over his hip, angled himself, and pushed. The dome of his cock slipped past her slick folds and he sank himself inside her, inch by agonizing inch. William tried to hold himself back, to go slow, but Poppy's knees squeezed around him and urged him on. *Now. Faster.* Before he knew it, he was completely buried inside her. He groaned and let his head drop onto her shoulder once more.

"God," she breathed. "Finally. That feels so *good."*

"You're the one who feels amazing, Poppy," William breathed. "Better than I could have imagined."

"So you imagined us," she panted defiantly. "I knew it!"

"So did you."

She didn't protest, and she definitely didn't argue when William started to rock against her. The couch sank a little more beneath them, but he barely noticed. The springs squeaked with their combined weight, but the noise barely registered. He lost himself in the sensation of her. He rolled his hips and thrust deeper, and she received him with a happy sigh. "William," she moaned his name again, and his own moan joined with hers. He had always been as stoic in the bedroom as he was in the board-room, but somehow William couldn't help it. He could control the movements of his body, but not its response to her.

He thrust into her slowly, rhythmically. He watched the progression of her pleasure. Her head fell back, her eyes fluttered closed. When her explosive little breaths and kittenish mewls weren't enough, he began to thrust harder. He needed more. He craved to know her every response. The sofa squeaked a louder protest. Poppy's breasts bounced more quickly beneath him. William leaned in until his chest pinned her own.

"Poppy," he moaned. He had pleasured himself so many times these past weeks imagining her this way. It was only now, in the heat of the moment, that he could fully admit it to himself. In his private moments he was consumed by his thoughts of her.

"Ohhh! Fuck, William!" Poppy cried. Her lips were parted, her teeth bared. There was perspiration beading her temple and darkening the blonde, tangled locks of her hair. William scooped his arms beneath her and gripped her close. His hips pumped into her like they had a mind of their own. Her thigh clenched around him...he felt caught in a vice...and all the while he submerged himself in the unbearable hot *tightness* of her. Now that he knew it, he couldn't bring himself to leave it for long. Every withdrawal segued to a harder, deeper thrust. He was pretty sure the violence of their lovemaking had already burst one of the couch cushions. One of Poppy's arms shot out to grope for something to hold onto, and the coffee table ground out a low note as she accidentally thrust it from her. The flailing arm eventually came to wrap around his neck again.

"William, I'm going to come!" she cried out.

William growled in throaty response. He wanted to challenge her to hold out as much as he wanted to dare her to do it, but he could feel his own orgasm building up inside him now. His thrusts came quicker; the slap of flesh against flesh was as loud as it was indecent as it was arousing as hell. His pulse roared in his ears as his heart sped out of control. He sank himself in Poppy and she cried wildly for everything: for him to speed up, for him to slow down, for him to give her a moment, for him to *not stop.* If her thoughts were scattering, then so was his ability to reason out what she was saying.

When she came, he felt it. Every limb wrapped around him clenched, and her whole body shuddered beneath him. She tensed as she built herself up...and up...and *up* to the unbearable point of climax, and then she spilled over with a wail. Her depths contracted around him, squeezing him, and William came unexpectedly. He ejaculated on an inward thrust; his hot seed spurted inside her. He stilled himself as he emptied every last drop. Then he sagged down on top of her, utterly spent. Once she had caught her breath again, Poppy laughed and pushed weakly at his dead weight, but she didn't demand that he move. William was grateful. He needed a minute to collect himself after the mind-blowing sex he had just experienced. It had been unplanned. It had been impulsive.

It had been absolutely incredible.

Afterward, once they had roused themselves to clean off and shower, William lay back in Poppy's bed and gazed into the unfamiliar shadows of her ceiling. He caught himself trying to memorize, again and again, every detail of the room…the moment…. He consoled himself with the knowledge this wouldn't be his last visit, not by any stretch of the imagination.

But it was that same comfort that worried him.

He wasn't an idiot. He knew he shouldn't have allowed things to get this far with Poppy. Sex and work, especially with your rival, definitely did *not* mix—yet somehow he kept finding himself in these situations with the feisty CEO of Wildflower Agency. Their night together seemed like a natural conclusion to the tension that had always existed between them.

But now what?

We'll keep it separate, William thought. *We're both professionals. It shouldn't be that hard to draw a line and agree to it.* He was starting to feel drowsy, and he was satisfied with his solution…for now. He wasn't one to procrastinate normally, but he didn't mind putting this particular puzzle off until tomorrow. He tilted his chin. The crown of Poppy's head rested beneath him; he watched it rise and fall with each breath he took. She looked completely relaxed, completely undisturbed by the fact that her biggest business rival was currently lying naked in her bed.

"I have a confession," he said after a while.

"Mmm?" Poppy stirred against his side and nuzzled closer. His hand came up to stroke the fine hair at her temple; then he let his fingers trace downward to tilt her chin toward him. Her eyes were half-closed, and he wasn't sure she was awake enough to hear his sin.

"I absolutely know what 'Netflix and Chill' means," he said. "Did you really think the CEO of *Jameson Ad Agency* would be out of the loop on that one?"

Poppy's eyes snapped open. She surged upward in his arms to stare at him. She looked for all the world like a post-orgasmic woman who had just learned she had sex with a complete surprise cloaked in her usual lover's clothes.

William grinned, and Poppy burst out laughing. She smacked his shoulder, and when she couldn't resist trying to hit him again, William pulled her in for a kiss.

CHAPTER EIGHT

POPPY

Poppy normally wasn't one to kiss and tell. She liked to keep her private life, well...private.

But after that hot night spent in William's arms, the lines between 'personal' and 'professional' had irrevocably blurred. She needed to get a handle on it, and fast.

So she called another impromptu meeting.

"Ugh, sis. This is gross. You realize how gross this is, right?" The voice of her older brother, Tristan, chastised her from the other end of the line. Poppy traded her cell phone to the other shoulder as she unlocked her car. It was the Sunday after her "sleepover" with William, and she was headed into the office early. She needed some time alone to work through plans for the convention. Even with William taking the lead, she hadn't forgotten that Wildflower was competing with Jameson Agency for the contract...or at least, she had forced herself to remember as much this morning. It was easier now that she was once more waking up to an empty space beside her in bed.

"Is the fact that I slept with William Jameson gross? Or the fact that I called you about my sex life gross?" she wondered.

"That last one. I don't know. The first one!"

"Let's just get one thing straight. William Jameson is *not* gross," she emphasized.

"I know." Tristan sighed gustily into the receiver. Poppy winced and pulled the phone away from her ear. "If I'm being honest, every guy I know in this city has a man-crush on one Jameson brother or another. Rich, handsome, successful…I hate them as much as I want to adopt a baby with one of them."

"What am I going to do?" Poppy asked mournfully. "He's my *nemesis,* Tristan!"

"It's a fine line between love and hate," he quoted. The reminder was needless at this point. "Do you think you can keep work and…the rest of it…separate?"

"No," Poppy moaned. "I don't know. *Help* me, Tristan Hanniford. You're my only hope."

"I'm going to try, sis. But I'm afraid if he was quoting Rhett Butler at you, things might be too far-gone already. I know better than anyone how much you loved that movie growing up." She could hear Tristan pulling a face at the memory. "You subjected me to it practically every day."

"What am I supposed to do now that the real-life Rhett Butler has shown up to sweep me off my feet?"

"Are you sure this guy is Rhett in this metaphor?" Tristan asked. "Because you always struck me as the 'Rhett' in any given relationship, Pops. You're the charming and supportive one, who somehow still manages to get shit done in the process...you have to admit Rhett is a better fit for you."

"I always thought I was Scarlett," Poppy muttered as she drove. Tristan couldn't be right. He *couldn't* be. Scarlett O'Hara was her girlhood hero: a strong female character who didn't need a man like Rhett, despite how perfectly suited he was for her. Wasn't that the moral of the story? If what Tristan said was true, then everything she had ever thought about herself seemed suddenly turned on its head.

"I think William might be the Scarlett in this case," Tristan said. He sounded sympathetic. "He's headstrong, take-charge."

"I can be those things too!" Poppy exclaimed.

"I think you're wonderful exactly the way you are, Pops. Sure, you could stand to promote your own agenda occasionally...okay, *more* than occasionally. But the great thing about you is the way you use your strength to support other people and raise everyone up together. I just don't want to see you get swept up in William Jameson's agenda at your own expense," Tristan said.

Poppy pulled into the parking garage below the agency and got out. She mentally chewed over everything her brother had said as she clicked up the concrete stairs to her office. Reception was poor in the garage, which afforded her some time to think about what her next protest to her brother's claims would be... but what wound up coming out of her mouth wasn't a protest at all.

"Okay. So I'm Rhett," she admitted as she let herself into the lobby. "I guess it's good to know the role I'm playing in all this. But it's more than William I have to worry about, Tristan. You remember that intern I was having trouble placing?"

"Emo Kid?" Tristan supplied. "I've been wondering about him! Did you fire him yet?"

"No. And I think that's becoming more of a problem than I've been willing to admit to myself." Poppy sighed heavily. She unlocked the door to the Wildflower Agency office and walked in. She immediately gravitated over toward Emo Kid's desk... and was unsurprised to find it in complete disarray. A cursory glance told her that the unfiled, water-stained papers on top of the heap were from at least three different projects, and two of those projects she had taken him from already.

"Sounds like you're doing an okay job of admitting it now," Tristan pointed out. "Maybe you just need to figure out what steps you need to take to pull the trigger."

Poppy grimaced. "I'm not taking him out back to put him out of his misery, Tristan."

"Yeah, that was kind of tactless. My bad. Still, you need to start framing this as a problem requiring a permanent solution rather than a temporary one, Pops. I know!" His excitement caused her to hold the phone away from her ear again. "You said yourself that this situation requires Scarlett tactics... and let's just admit to ourselves those are skills you might not have necessarily acquired yet. Why don't you go to William with your problem and see what he says?"

"William?" Poppy repeated uncertainly. Just hearing the name conjured an image of what he would do if he was in a similar situation…and Tristan was right. William *would* approach the problem with Emo Kid differently. He would have no problem calling him out on his bad haircuts and unprofessional workplace fashion; hell, William wouldn't have even let it get to this point. He would have sent the kid on his way with a curt farewell—and *maybe* a fairly-worded letter of recommendation—after the first colossal screw-up. "…I don't know," she muttered. "It doesn't feel fair to Emo Kid. He's *my* employee."

"First of all, listen to yourself. Does this intern even have a name? You've been dehumanizing and distancing yourself from him from the beginning."

"I have not!"

Tristan chuckled. "You're right, that was unfair of me. I'm just saying you do have Scarlett instincts, Poppy, it's just not in your nature to act on them. Don't think of this as a blot on your character. You know what needs to be done, and if William is available to help you do it, why not take advantage of the resource?"

Poppy chewed her lower lip between her teeth as she pondered Tristan's words. "I don't want to delegate this," she reiterated. "But maybe you're right. Maybe I should ask for William's advice."

"And you need an excuse to see him again," Tristan provided helpfully. "One that isn't personal."

She sighed. "I hate it when you're right all the time."

"It's a tough racket being the smarter older brother," he lamented.

"Goodbye smartass. I'm hanging up now."

"Love you, sister. Whether you're a Scarlett or a Rhett. And you're definitely a Rhett," he said quickly as Poppy thumbed the call to a close. She shook her head, smiling ruefully to herself. Calls with Tristan always felt eventful, and she usually came away from them with more insight into herself...for better or for worse.

"All right, William," she breathed as she sat down at her desk and opened her laptop to send the e-mail. "You're my Scarlett. Let's see what you got."

CHAPTER NINE

WILLIAM

"You," William said incredulously. *"You* want to fire someone."

Poppy squirmed in his office chair. He had given her complete authority to sit behind his desk, mainly because he thought he would enjoy the sight of her on his 'throne' (as she liked to call it), but Poppy had never taken him up on the offer until today. It was Monday evening, and she had called his office to see if he was still in...likely knowing that this was precisely where she would find him, he suspected. She hadn't wasted any time in driving over and collapsing into his big leather office chair when he offered it today.

"No, I don't want to fire anyone!" she protested. "I'm just... I'm in a bit of a bind, is all. I need some other ideas for what my options are."

"Let me guess," William said as he crossed to the liquor cabinet. "Not only have you never fired anyone before, but your idea of 'firing' involves finding your employee a new position at another company. That position is likely a promotion over what they had with you, and pays more. Have you ever actually notified anyone they were terminated?"

Poppy pulled a face. "'Terminated'. Ugh. I hate that word. Why is business-speak so...murderous-sounding? It's just advertising!"

"'Just advertising'," William repeated with a chuckle. He poured them both a glass of amber-colored scotch and carried one over to her. Poppy accepted without really noticing and took a long sip. He loved the way her lush lips wrapped around the glass, the elegant way her throat worked as she swallowed. Just watching her now made the front of William's pants tighten, but he wasn't about to interrupt her work problem with his own personal urgency.

Not until he helped her find the solution, anyway.

"You're right," she sighed. "Advertising is what I live for. *Good* advertising."

"It's what we both live for. And it's what the people who work for you should passionately pursue." William leaned back against his desk and crossed his arms, cradling his glass meditatively. "Who are you trying to cut loose? Someone I know?"

"Again, not trying to cut anyone loose, per se," Poppy corrected him. "But the person in question is...someone who's made himself a bit infamous," she admitted. "It's Emo Kid. He..."

William's fingers clenched over his glass. He didn't think he was in danger of breaking it, but he set it aside after a moment just in case. "He's the one who tied the knot that almost got you killed," he said darkly. "Poppy, what the hell is he still doing at your company?"

"It was an honest mistake outside of his regular duties," she put in defensively. "Seriously, William. Anyone could have tied that knot incorrectly."

"His oversight doesn't begin nor end there, and you know it," he reminded her. He was having trouble keeping his temper in check in the wake of this revelation, but he knew he needed to tamp down the flame a bit, at least until she was gone. His fury wasn't for Poppy. "The knot just so happens to be the least forgivable offense in a long string of them. Someone could have been seriously injured because of his gross negligence. I had expected you to fire him the moment we made it back from the course."

"Well..." Poppy swirled her glass and stared very hard at the surface of his desk. "... that might be why I came to you. I'm not beyond asking for help. I know I get in my own way sometimes when it comes to my employees. I'm just not sure what to do in this case, and I need to look at multiple solutions. I was hoping you could help me think outside my own box. I *am* set in my ways when it comes to handling things like this...but I'm starting to realize it might not always be good for business."

William's face softened as he took her in. She was a strong woman, and a strong leader within her company—of this he had never had any doubt. But observing the way she sat here now, slouched and looking vulnerable in her abject misery, was telling of how big her heart was. Of course she would struggle with something like this. How could she not? She valued her employees more than anyone William had ever met. Other ad execs, himself included, were ruthless in the way they conducted business. Poppy Hanniford was decidedly *not* ruthless, and her empathetic take on the human side of things was humbling.

But she didn't need his reassurances now. What she required was his method. When those gorgeous green eyes of hers finally glanced his way, sad but hopeful, it was like a shock to his system. He had never felt so strongly that he needed to intervene on another's behalf. It was a feeling similar to the one he had felt the day Poppy had almost plummeted forty feet right before his eyes. Just thinking about it was enough to make his blood boil again, but he needed to stay calm. He needed to execute a plan, swiftly and precisely, to make sure this sort of thing never happened again.

"I see what's needed here," he reassured her. "Give me the evening to think this over. By tomorrow I should have the solution for you." He picked up his scotch again and held it in a commiserating toast. Poppy hesitated, then smiled. She leaned across the desk to clink her glass against his.

"I really appreciate your input, William. Seriously. Anything you can do. Including a refill," she hinted as she sat back in the chair. William smiled and rose, offering his hand, and she handed him her empty glass gratefully.

A refill is the least I can do for you, he thought. *But you're right, Poppy. I will do anything.*

William acted on schedule, as promised, although he didn't devote as much thought as he had implied before executing his plan. He knew exactly how he would put it into motion before Poppy left his office. He fulfilled his promise Tuesday.

Poppy was in his office again Wednesday morning.

"William!" She burst through the door in a flurry of blonde hair and billowing purple pea coat. William saw a snapshot of his secretary standing ineffectually, her arm outstretched, just before the door slammed shut behind Poppy. The blonde crossed to his desk in a fury…a fury, safe to say, that William had not been expecting. He mastered his astonished look before she arrived at his desk. He held out his hand to her, but she stopped short of accepting the offered chair. She glared at him.

The silence that followed her stormy entry was deafening, but Poppy eventually broke it. "Tell me you didn't." Her voice was almost a whisper. *"Please* tell me that you didn't fire my employee."

"Don't be absurd." It was the wrong thing to say. It was too defensive. Poppy's eyes narrowed, but she offered no immediate argument. She waited. "Poppy, of course I didn't fire someone from *your* agency. All I did was express my strong wish for his removal from our shared project. He was a threat to the work, and to the cohesion of the team…not to mention completely irresponsible when it came to checking his work when it was *your* life on the line."

"You knew exactly what would happen!" Poppy hissed. William felt certain that if there wasn't a desk between them in that moment, she would be stabbing his chest with her finger. "I saw the memo you wrote to my project manager! You bullied her into taking him off the project and advising him to find employment in another industry. She used *your* words! He quit without so much as speaking to me, and without even a letter of recommendation!"

"You should have never considered writing him one," William said. "Poppy...Poppy!" he snapped when she turned away from him. He bounded out from behind his desk and grabbed her by the shoulders to prevent her from leaving. She swayed slightly in place as he turned her around, but made no move to pull free from him. He didn't know if he should feel encouraged. Her eyes were green fire, and he had never seen a woman more ready to reduce him to ash. "Poppy, I did exactly what we discussed! I took care of it for you. I don't understand this reception."

"*We* didn't discuss *any* of this, William! What I wanted was someone to support me while I made difficult decisions that had to do with my own company...my own life!" she exclaimed. "I didn't want you to take charge! Is that really what you thought?"

"I..." William didn't have a ready response. In truth, he hadn't put much thought into it at all. As soon as Poppy had described her problem, he had zeroed in on the solution and implemented it. "I was just trying to protect you." The explanation sounded so weak, so facile, but Poppy didn't appear angry or resentful. She was peering at him intently. William gazed back at her. He wondered if she could see it replaying behind his eyes: the moment on the ropes course, the moment he almost lost her. It had been all he could think about. *If I hadn't been near you, if I hadn't been prepared to shoulder our weight, if my climbing skills had been inadequate...if it were to happen again...*

"Protect me from what, William?" Her voice was quieter. "From having to make hard decisions? They're *my* hard decisions. You wouldn't respect me as an equal if you thought I couldn't handle myself. So do you?"

"Do I what?"

"Do you respect me?" she demanded.

"Of course I respect you." He didn't need to think. "I more than respect you. Poppy, of course I know you're capable."

"Then you better start acting like it," she warned as she stepped out of his arms. "We're a team, William. If I come to you, it means I trust you enough to want your advice. I *want* your support. But I'm afraid your management style isn't going to work in this partnership...professional or otherwise. So I'll see you at the convention Friday," she concluded as she took a step back.

"You'll see me," William promised.

"Good. Because in light of recent events, I've made some last-minute changes to our costumes. You'll be getting an e-mail from me today," Poppy mentioned over her shoulder as she departed. "I'm throwing down the gauntlet, so be ready."

"Better than impaling me on it," William muttered. He watched her walk out, wishing he didn't so enjoy the mesmerizing sway of that tight, trim posterior. Whatever she would be wearing to the convention, he had no doubt that she would look damn good filling it.

After she had vanished back out the door, William relaxed a

little. He hadn't realized he'd been grinding his teeth, but it was better to clamp down on what he really wanted to say then let the words pour forth. How could Poppy not see that he had done this for her? What's more, what he had done had flown in the face of his own self-interest. Jameson Agency looked better if Wildflower had incompetents on staff. He had only sought to do her a favor by helping her cull her staff and make it more efficient. It was something *he* was good at, and hadn't she come to him seeking his expertise?

He moved back around to his desk and sat down. He was unsurprised to find an unopened e-mail from Wildflower Agency at the top of his inbox.

He clicked it open and braced himself.

CHAPTER TEN

POPPY

If her arrival at the convention was something of a sensation, then Poppy couldn't wait to see the reception that William was going to get.

"Oh, Miss Hanniford! You look absolutely gorgeous." One of the authors on their panel, a mousy woman who hadn't spoken more than three words to her over the course of their meetings, came running over the moment she clapped eyes on Poppy. "Holy crap. What an innovative idea to switch up your choice of costume!"

"You like it?" Poppy executed a little turn to show off her ensemble. She wore a sleek black suit and choker, her honey-blonde locks straightened and slicked-back. She had indulged herself in a little smoky eye makeup and scarlet lip color to soften the masculine choice of costume.

"Almost as dreamy as the original Rhett Butler," her admirer enthused. "This *so* fits with the 'unconventional' theme of our panel! Everyone's going to want to know who the crossdressing Rhett Butler is repping. Although..." The author glanced around curiously, and Poppy knew her question before she asked it. "Is Mr. Jameson partnering with you in your cosplay?"

"That remains to be seen." Poppy couldn't help the amusement that colored her tone. It was the exact challenge she had posed to William earlier that week: in sticking with their theme of turning romance conventions on their head, she had informed him of her intention to come dressed as *Gone with the Wind's* hero. That left him with only one option if he wanted to match her idea.

If you insist on being such a Scarlett, then you can dress the part, Poppy thought mischievously. She was lost in her vision of William draped in a dress—and her suspicion that he might not follow through at all, which she would take as a personal victory —when the author she was speaking to tapped her on the shoulder. She pointed excitedly toward the entrance of the convention center, and Poppy turned, her heart already climbing into her throat in anticipation.

It was William, all right, and he had *not* disappointed. He wasn't wearing the full-on gown that Poppy had envisioned, but that didn't mean he had taken the 'vision' part out of the equation. William was dressed in an emerald green brocade suit that was completely evocative of Scarlett's infamous curtain dress. When he turned to address the cluster of overexcited authors that came to meet him, Poppy could clearly see the coat's exaggerated tails —from behind, it was *almost* dress-like. Poppy waited to greet him, fighting a smile. She could see his eyes skimming over the heads of the crowd to locate her. His look when he saw her was approving...*more* than approving. She loved the way his eyes darkened even more when he focused on her.

He said his farewells cordially, even dropping a little bow to his fans. As if he could get anymore swoon-worthy in that getup. He moved toward Poppy and she met him halfway.

"Frankly, my dear, you look damn amazing," Poppy said in her best sultry baritone.

"I would reply with my passionate refusal to never go hungry again, but it would be a bald-faced lie, " William said. "You look utterly edible in that outfit." William said. He leaned in. "I've never had more of an appetite for anyone in my life."

A shiver of pleasure coursed through her at his words. The heat of his breath on the back of her neck was almost enough to undo her right then and there. She had worked too hard on pulling together her Rhett costume to rip it all off for William now. Instead, she offered him her arm. "Walk with me to the panel?"

William surprised her for the second time that evening by accepting her lead, before swiftly executing a maneuver that turned her around and pulled her into the crook of *his* arm. Poppy laughed despite herself. Of course William couldn't stand to let someone else take the lead...but in this case, she thought she would allow it. Their own individual experience was bound to be full of these little power plays. She personally couldn't wait to get the upper hand on him again.

"William! Poppy!" The author leading their panel bustled over. "We're about ready to start! We were wondering if the two of you would like to say a few words of introduction to kick us off?"

Poppy glanced at William as they entered the room together. She hadn't prepared anything, but she wasn't afraid to wing it. William raised an eyebrow at her, and she thought they were on the same wavelength. "Not at all," she told the lead panelist. "We're happy to do it."

"Great!" The author looked immensely relieved, and Poppy wasn't unsympathetic. So many of the authors they had worked closely with over the past few weeks were decidedly not public speakers, and they would be the first to admit it themselves. Someone used to giving presentations could easily break the ice for them so they could go forward with their talking points.

William pulled out one of the chairs at the main table for Poppy, and she accepted. It felt in-character for them to conduct themselves grandly, even around the panel. It was only when she noticed that William had remained standing that she realized he intended to speak first.

"Welcome, everyone, to Conventional Romance," he said. His resonant voice carried, and the audience immediately hushed. "I would love to pose a question before we start. What does it mean to be conventional?" he asked. "Besides its usage here as a clever pun." Several people chuckled in agreement. The audience was starting to relax, and Poppy could feel the energy in the room turn in his favor. It was remarkable, really, how easily William assumed command. "We all have our individual definitions of the word...of what we personally find conventional. Convention is expected; ordinary; *safe*. Convention has its place and serves a purpose. Old formulas, tried and true tropes… they have all been proven to work before, and we know they will work again."

William paused, and Poppy half-rose. She could sense the beats of his speech, and she was eager to pick up his flow. "…but if you know what works, then so does your audience," William continued. Poppy froze. Her ass hovered above her seat, and she eased back down again slowly. She didn't think anyone noticed that she had made to stand, least of all William. She came home to roost and crossed her arms impatiently. "They've seen it all before," William said. "And they crave something new. Something *different.* Even if what you offer is a new spin on an old favorite."

The audience in the front row leaned in to whisper appreciatively to one another. Poppy distinctly heard talk of their costumes…along with talk of William.

She took a long sip of water from one of the provided bottles. Her chest suddenly felt tight, and she didn't know why. The suit hugged her bust, but it wasn't *that* constrictive…so why was it suddenly harder to breathe? *He didn't take credit for your idea, Poppy,* she reminded herself. *And you don't need credit, anyway. The costumes are just for fun. They were for the two of you to put on a show.*

Then why does it suddenly feel like you were never given the script?

"At Jameson Ad Agency, we reject the conventional," William said. He turned and gestured to Poppy. "The partnership Miss Hanniford and I formed came unexpectedly, and I wouldn't have it any other way. We hope to spend the weekend promoting our definition of what it means to be *unconventional.*"

Poppy made to rise again.

"So thank you, Conventional Romance," William concluded. "I look forward to meeting with many of you in the coming days. In the meantime, I pass things off to the panel. It's what we're all here for." A handsome grin drew his intro to a perfect close. William sat down amidst a smattering of applause. Poppy's jaw clenched so tightly she thought her teeth would crack. When William's thigh brushed against her own beneath the table, she wanted to knock it away.

"Great speech." She wished the compliment didn't sound so forced, but William didn't appear to notice. He made a minor adjustment to his brocade. He was still beaming from ear to ear.

"I figured something short and semi-poetic would start us off strong. Sorry I forgot to plug Wildflower. Sometimes the fact that our agencies have teamed-up still gets away from me." He tried to move his hand to her knee reassuringly beneath the table, but Poppy pulled it away.

Frankly, my dear, she thought, *I don't think you give a damn.*

CHAPTER ELEVEN

WILLIAM

William sat in the publisher's waiting room. His leg jogged. He stilled it.

It was hard not to recall that he had first met Poppy in this room, and that he had watched as one of her slender legs jogged similarly. He could see now that it wasn't a nervous habit to be suppressed, but one that spoke of boundless, positive energy. So much of that energy had resided within Poppy from the very beginning. He regretted that it had taken him until now to see it for what it was, and to know how infectious it could be.

A lot had changed for him since meeting Poppy.

William glanced at the clock posted on the wall. They were five minutes out from getting called into the final meeting with the publishing company, and Poppy was nowhere to be seen. She wasn't responding to any of his texts; William had limited himself to three, and even that felt excessive for him, but the delay in her arrival also felt excessive. Poppy always arrived as early to an appointment as he did. A nagging worry continued to invade his thoughts—*what if something happened to her on the way over*—but he pushed it stubbornly from his mind. He would deal with the reality of an accident if and only if it came to pass. He wouldn't waste any excess energy on worrying about the worst.

Somehow, this private affirmation didn't stop the thought from invading his brain again a few minutes later.

He tried to concentrate instead on the presentation he intended to give. The publishing house was scheduled to make their final decision today on who would get the campaign, and William intended to make that decision for them. He had it all laid out: how he would insist on speaking first, before anyone else, and how he would take command of the center of the room. Poppy would be surprised, but he wouldn't leave her in suspense for long. She should know that she'd won; that he agreed with her now what winning truly was. He intended to tell the publishing company exactly what they would be missing out on if they decided to award their business to only one agency. His proposal would put both Jameson and Wildflower at the helm; he would emphasize, with all the data he had collected to back up his claim, that they worked best as a team. He would even take a pay cut to ensure that they continued on this course, and he had no doubt that Poppy would be willing to do the same…besides, he was confident in his ability to renegotiate the pay after. Right now, all that mattered was that the project continued to move forward with the same incredible momentum they had already amassed.

All that mattered was that he continue to work alongside Poppy Hanniford. It was important for his own agency's growth, and…it was important for him. As a leader, and as a man who had fallen head-over-heels in love. He didn't intend to include that last part in his presentation, but it was something he intended to relay to her later, in private.

The clock struck the appointed hour of the meeting, and the door opened. William's leg had started jogging again without him realizing it, and he mastered the tic now that he had an audience; he rose, pocketing the thumb drive that contained his presentation, and prepared his best apologetic smile. He had no problem stalling for time and blaming traffic for Poppy's delay….

…but it was Poppy he saw now, walking out of the room with their clients. She paused in the hallway to shake hands with the company's representative, and William froze as he watched her. She was smiling, although her eyes seemed a little tighter than usual. Her lips were forming words of gratitude, but she looked distinctly unhappy about it…at least, William thought he could see all the cues.

He knew without being informed what had just happened in that room, but he still couldn't believe what he was seeing. Poppy disengaged the handshake, her eyes moving to him, but William refused contact. He didn't want to infer anymore; he wanted to be told. He strolled into the room and waited for the representative to close the door behind them.

"You've given the campaign to Wildflower," he said. It wasn't a question.

The head smiled sympathetically and laced her hands. "Yes,"

she agreed. "I'm sorry, Mr. Jameson. Ms. Hanniford requested to come early and talk with us more about her vision for the project. We appreciate what your agency brought to the table, but we preferred Ms. Hanniford's planned approach. Her ideas are ambitious, like yours, but they are also more out-of-the-box. We were excited by what she has to offer. And at the end of the day, her vision was simply more team-oriented, and more in line with what our company is looking for."

"Team-oriented," William repeated. The thumb drive felt heavy in his pocket with the weight of the irony of her statement. "I see."

"I'm sorry, Mr. Jameson. Our company really did enjoy working with you, but it simply wasn't a perfect fit for us. Not without Wildlfower. I hated having to make the decision more than I thought I would." The representative shook her head. "I really hope we can work together again in the very near future."

The meeting concluded quickly. As soon as the door had closed, and he was alone in the hallway, William strode for the elevators. He had intended to try and catch Poppy before she left, but he was still surprised to find her chatting with the receptionist in the hallway. Her eyes leapt to him, and she didn't appear surprised that his own meeting had concluded so soon. It was almost enough to make him wonder if she had been waiting for him.

"Miss Hanniford, do you mind if I ride with you?"

Poppy maintained her smile, but he saw the tension still hanging around her eyes. "Not at all, Mr. Jameson. Please." She indicated the elevator as it opened, and William allowed her to step in first. He followed her and punched the door closed behind them. He didn't designate a floor, and neither did Poppy. They both knew what this impromptu meeting was about.

"Wow. You're really furious at me." Poppy seemed surprised by whatever she saw in his face.

William could feel his fist clenching and unclenching itself at his side, as if it was hoping to catch hold of the exact words he wanted to use in this situation. He forced it to still. When he thought he could speak evenly again, he risked his next words. "Forgive me, Poppy, but this is the third client your agency has stolen out from under mine."

"Stolen?" she echoed incredulously. "William, we were in competition with each other!"

"We weren't," he seethed. "You *know* that we weren't. Don't play games with me now. There's no one in this elevator, or in this conversation, but you and I. So drop the damn act already."

"The act?" she demanded. "What act? I'm not the one who was *acting* like this was a job competition all along! *You* were! You were always putting your agency—no, not your agency, *yourself*—first! And by being supportive of you, I was getting left in the dust. You took advantage of me, and I..." Poppy sucked in a hard breath and appeared to compose herself. William stared at her, stricken by what she was saying. Fearing what she would say next. "...I let you walk all over me," she concluded finally. "It's my fault things were turning out the way they were. But don't for a second think that by taking charge of my own destiny I somehow *slighted* you. Don't you dare *accuse* me of underhanded tactics, or of not being a team player. I played fair this entire time. But we were playing by different rules, William. And I figured out, finally, that I was playing at a disadvantage."

He wanted to speak. He wanted to defend himself against her claims, but no words came. His head was empty except for the reverberations of her words; his throat was dry as dust. "...I'm sorry if I operated in a way that gave you that impression," he said finally. "Truly, I thought we were in this together."

Poppy crossed her arms, and turned slightly toward the corner of the elevator. "You wanted to lead," she said finally. "It's what you're good at. But it's also become apparent to me that it's *all* you know. And when a person leads like you do, they often forget to check in with everyone else to see if they're following. You're Atlas: you want to take the world on your shoulders. It's a trait of yours that I l...that I admire. More than I can express. But the person I want to align myself with should be able to meet me halfway. They should want to support me as much as I support them."

Poppy pressed the button for the lobby. William stared at the glowing light, wishing he could come up with an idea that was equally brilliant in that moment. Something that would return things to the way they were. Something that would win her back.

"The presentation I was going to make today..." William cut himself off as the elevator door opened. He didn't know what good an undelivered presentation would do him now. Poppy blinked; she didn't walk immediately out of the elevator. She waited for him to continue.

But William did not continue.

"I'm sure it would have been excellent," she said finally. "Your presentations usually are. Goodbye, William."

No, he thought as he watched her walk out into the lobby. *It would have been unlike any presentation I've ever given before.*

"Goodbye, Poppy," he said quietly. The elevator doors closed over his farewell.

CHAPTER TWELVE

E-MAIL DATED: Monday A.M.
SUBJECT: The Future of the Project

Miss Hanniford:
    I take it by now you have also met with your staff and arrived at the same conclusions I have. I found that, despite the contract being awarded to Wildflower Agency, it appears our employees have taken the liberty of comingling and forming teams to tackle various aspects of the campaign. Please advise me of how you would like to proceed given the circumstances.

Congratulations again on the campaign. I know you will do creditable work as always.

Respectfully,
William Jameson

∾

Mr. Jameson:

Thank you for your e-mail. I do appreciate the amount of work we will have going forward in untangling our staffs. It appears that things are just as you perceived: there isn't a single team that assembled itself that *isn't* comprised of both Jameson and Wildflower employees.

In the preparations for the convention I admit that I didn't dissuade, but rather encouraged, my employees to collaborate with your own. I thought we could achieve our best work that way and I wasn't wrong. However, I apologize for the confusion this has created for your team.

If you agree to it, then at this time, I think the best course of action for the good of the project would be to continue with the teams staffed as they are. Jameson Ad Agency will of course be compensated for the time. Your employees bring a uniform excellence to their work that I must credit to your strength as their leader.

Thank you for your congratulations. I intend to do *outstanding* work, as always.

Respectfully,

Poppy Hanniford

~

E-MAIL DATED: Wednesday P.M.

SUBJECT: Re: The Future of the Project

Miss Hanniford:

I appreciate your compliment, but I believe I have learned more about true leadership after a few weeks with you than I have during a lifetime of service to my agency.

Indeed, I would like to apologize to you. You were right in your criticisms of me, and perhaps even right to the contract alone when you believed we could not work together. I've been told all my life that a shrewd and forceful personality is the only way to succeed in getting what I want--that opposition only exists to be crushed, and that anything else is weakness.

But I've also been taught repeatedly in recent days that exerting my will without regard for others isn't just dangerous for my business relationships, but also my personal ones. It's a short-sighted way to live.

My strength is also my weakness. In the end, it drove the thing I wanted most away.

I regret the way things ended between us. I regret my behavior most of all. I regret that things are so busy that I have been unable to reach you at your office.

I'm not a man of many regrets.

Yours respectfully,

William Jameson

∾

E-MAIL DATED: Sunday A.M.

Mr. Jameson:

I accept your apology. Thank you. More than that, I had hoped to deliver my own.

I want to apologize for the harsh words I used outside the meeting with the publishing house. I don't usually lose my temper like that, and in hindsight I feel that I was out of line myself. Tensions ran high with this particular interview, as you know, but that was not an excuse for my behavior.

I hope the coming week finds you well. I look forward to working together to iron out the kinks with our staff. You employ good people and instill a solid work ethic in your staff. My own team can only be enhanced from working closely with them, no matter how briefly.

Thank you again, and my apologies that it took until the weekend to get back to you. I've had a lot on my mind.

Yours respectfully,

Poppy Hanniford

~

E-MAIL DATED: Sunday P.M.
SUBJECT: The Future

William,

I realize now that a formal apology isn't enough from me, and it isn't enough *for* me. In fact, rereading what I wrote, it rings completely hollow and inadequate, and it's almost enough to make me wish I had never hit 'send'. But I know that an apology to you is necessary.

So please allow me to try again.

I need my apology to be personal to you. You've come to mean more to me than I can ever hope to express in a box of text...and more than I ever successfully expressed to you in person.

I got caught up in competing. I got caught up in the work. More than that, I got caught up in all the things that I perceived *weren't* working. I didn't look at the bigger picture of you and me. I saw how strong you were, how formidable, but it never frightened or intimidated me. It woke me up to my own potential. It excited every fiber of my being to be near you, and to see that same response excited in you.

I wish I had communicated that better before it was gone.

And here we are now, *communicating,* and I still can't express what I feel when we are together...and what I feel for *you.* You are everything I never expected to find. And suddenly this work, and this city that I love, seem somehow less without your perspective. Your dynamism.

Your passion.

If you receive this e-mail, it will be in the aftermath of a long war with myself. I'm afraid that I've said too much.

But I'm more afraid of not saying enough.

Yours,

Poppy

CHAPTER THIRTEEN

POPPY

Three days. All communication between them had ceased for three days after her last e-mail, and the silence was deafening. What was William *thinking?* What was *she* thinking? Why had she even sent him that last message...?

...and what did William's early morning invitation to meet with him today really mean?

Poppy's head spun with questions she fought to order as she stepped out of the car. *Three days.* Was it possible that Jameson Ad Agency had added on additional floors in that time? She didn't remember the building being *this* intimidating. True, even on a sunny New York City day it looked like a front for the operations of some hyper-efficient supervillain.

...all right, so that wasn't *entirely* true. Poppy had liked to think so back before she came to know the Jameson family, but she couldn't look at it—any of it—the same way now. The building looked taller than she remembered, but she remembered it fondly. Stepping into its halls had once been as exhilarating as stepping out of her own reality and into another. She had felt the pulse of industry there; the thriving business culture; the race to be the *first* and *best,* and it had been an exhilarating feeling.

It had been a short-lived feeling.

She passed through the doors and walked directly to the elevators. She was headed for the top floor. William had asked for a meeting. Poppy had no idea what he wanted to discuss, but her only consolation was that calling a meeting was *so* William. It wasn't that there was any particular relief to be found in his predictability, but…it was a side of him she loved. Desperately. His love of business, and his forthrightness in requesting something he wanted—these were all traits that she admired the hell out of, and found herself missing already after the three-day silence. She punched the button for the top floor, and the doors closed over her.

"Go right in, Miss Hanniford." William's secretary barely glanced up from her computer screen when Poppy entered. It was only a little past six AM, and the poor woman looked as if the coffee mug steaming beside her had been brewed pitch black and flavored with Wishful Thinking.

"Thank you." Poppy pulled William's office door open and walked in.

He was sitting behind his desk. Poppy hadn't really expected to find him anywhere else. Her heart trembled at the sight of him, but all thoughts of being intimidated fled from her in that moment; she couldn't get over how goddamn good he looked, and how much she had missed seeing him in the flesh. His messages were as professional and as poised as he was, but they were no substitute for the man himself. William glanced up when she entered. His dark eyes held her, and she wasn't close enough to see the blue in them.

She walked forward.

"You're early," he said.

"So was your e-mail," she pointed out. "Four-thirty AM? I thought you were in another time zone at first."

"I couldn't sleep last night." If that was the case, then William certainly didn't wear his fatigue like most mortals. His dark hair held the usual effortless coif, and the perfect angularity of his jaw was as distinguished as always by his careful stubble. He motioned, unnecessarily, for her to sit down. Poppy sat in the visitor's chair and crossed her legs neatly. She hated having the massive desk divide them more than she expected.

Because how else had she imagined this meeting taking place?

"Do you need coffee?" she asked. She wanted to invite him out…across the street…anywhere but here where he had to inhabit the role of CEO so fully. But she lost her nerve. She jerked her head back the way she came and offered a little half-smile. "I think your secretary brewed every bean in the building."

William's mouth flexed. It was almost a smile of agreement. *Almost.* "I won't deny how tempting that sounds. But I'll wait. I've worked out a presentation I'd like to give you, and I'd like to give it now, before we get into why I called you here."

Poppy's heart sank as he rose. "That e-mail I sent…" she began. "I know I owe you more…so much more than…"

"You don't owe me anything." William flipped the light off and switched on the projector. "You don't even owe me an audience. You can walk out at any moment, Miss Hanniford. But I hope that you don't." William clicked over to the title slide.

Poppy Hanniford: A Presentation, the first slide read.

Poppy's jaw dropped. She quickly clamped it shut again. She kept her legs crossed, but held onto her knee to prevent it from jogging uncontrollably. She had wondered if a presentation might be involved in today's meeting, but she had never expected it to be about *her.*

"Poppy, even before I met you, I knew you were a formidable individual. Strong. Intelligent." William had his back to her as he spoke. He was looking at the presentation, but didn't appear to be reading off it. There wasn't much to read, anyway. He had bullet points listed, sure, but these were accompanied by photos: her professional headshot, the photographs taken of her as Rhett Butler... and candids. Poppy hadn't expected that. There were pictures of her smiling; pictures of her laughing; pictures where her green eyes appeared to be flaming (and William was often featured in these). But *she* was the focus of the presentation's media, and of the presentation itself.

"William..." She couldn't *not* say something, but she didn't know how to continue.

William carried on as if uninterrupted. "In the first draft of this presentation I included a slide about your beauty: your effortlessness, your radiance, your complete charm and natural magnetism."

Poppy wiped her eyes. William turned to her, and even in the shadowy glow of the presentation, she could see his expression clearly. It wasn't the imperious man behind the desk who was speaking to her now. It was the man she had come to know and love: private, sensitive, and powerful in the moments he let himself be so. "I won't deny that these traits are wonderful strengths, and intrinsic to you. But I decided that they can't be encompassed in a presentation. *You* can't be encompassed in a presentation, and don't think for a second I don't know that. But I need you to see what I see, Poppy. I need you to see what the *world* sees."

He seemed to be asking for permission to continue. Poppy nodded. The slides clicked by, one after the other, each highlighting a perceived strength of her character: her fiery temper, her supportiveness of others, her innovation and audacity and utter fearlessness of things new and untried. As William continued, Poppy realized it was no use wiping her face anymore. The tears flowed freely under cover of darkness in his office. William pitched to her the portrait of a woman who sounded invincible. She sounded like a storybook queen and knight and ad magic enchantress rolled all into one. When he began to wrap it all up with graphs comparing and contrasting their talents, and showing how they complemented one another in every sector, Poppy started to laugh. She couldn't help it. The feeling he had instilled her with was too wonderful for words.

"In conclusion, I identified that something was missing in all this," William stated. *"You* were missing something, Poppy. And that was your own Poppy. What you need is someone in your own court to act as cheerleader. A CEO of your talent and ambition and insight can't operate almost solely in support of others. Your good nature allows you to see potential everywhere you look, and to *act* on it... but the humility you carry with you, the same thing that allows you to put ego aside for the betterment of the project, is holding back your own potential. In order to achieve all that you were meant for, you need someone who is equally supportive of you and your ideas. I would like to be that person for you, Poppy."

The slideshow clicked to an end. The lights came back up. At the conclusion of the presentation, Poppy rose. She crossed to the window to gaze out at the city below. She swallowed audibly, trying to evict her heart from her throat.

"Miss Hanniford," William said. "Would you care for a glass of water? Coffee?"

"Scotch," she replied. She heard William chuckle appreciatively. She watched in the reflection off the glass as he crossed to his cabinet and pulled the little door open. He fished down two glasses and the most expensive-looking bottle in his collection.

"That was quite a presentation, Mr. Jameson," she said.

"Thank you, Miss Hanniford. I don't think I'm exaggerating when I say it's the most important one I've ever given."

She watched him pour their drinks in the window's mirror world. When hers was ready, she drew in a deep breath, and turned to face him. She accepted the glass, but she didn't drink immediately. They didn't toast. Even the ice cubes in her scotch seemed to be holding back on cracking. The air in the room was charged with anticipation.

"I want to propose a merger of sorts," William said.

Poppy's heart gave a hard *thump!* in her chest. She was surprised the throb didn't knock her completely off her feet. "A merger. Of sorts." *What are you, an echo? Say something else, Poppy!* "I must say that sounds intriguing, Mr. Jameson. I would love to know the terms of the merger you are proposing."

William gestured for her to sit—not in the chair reserved for his appointments, but against his desk. Beside him. Poppy crossed to join him. They both still held their untouched glasses aloft. William seemed to have forgotten he had poured them drinks at all.

"What I'm proposing," he said, "is that we merge our companies. Jameson and Wildflower. It's become more than apparent to me over the last few months that we are stronger together. That being said, I will happily continue to take on Wildflower as a rival—there are no other challengers out there that force us to put out our best work quite like you do."

"I agree," Poppy said. "Every fire requires a little friction to get started."

"But those forces don't have to be opposing to be effective," William continued quietly. "In fact, I think it's obvious that the combination has the potential to be harnessed. What we could build together, Poppy...we could lead the industry. You and I."

"Together," she repeated. "As partners?"

"As more," William said. He raised his glass. "Effective immediately I also suggest we create a focus group for an in-depth exploration of how you and I can merge most fully, with the greatest possible satisfaction given to both lovers."

The word on his lips...his tongue...she *had* to taste it. She clinked her glass against William's, then swooped in before he could take even a single sip of scotch. She caught his mouth with hers, plucking his surprised lower lip out of the air with her teeth, teasing it into position until she was kissing him fully. She heard the distant tinkle of ice as William set his drink down. Her hand came up to cup his cheek, to cement him in place; his alcohol may have been expensive, but she could drink *him* forever. Her lips roved, and he returned the pressure of her kiss with the heat and need she had been looking for. He took the liberty of removing the glass of scotch from her hand and setting it aside.

"Fuck. I'll take that as a 'yes'," William groaned against her.

"But how many times can you make me say the word?" Poppy asked with teasing innocence. She batted her eyes at him; their faces were pressed so closely together that her lashes swept against his cheek. "I'd be curious to know the sort of *prowess* that goes into your negotiations."

"I'd be happy to show you as many times as you like," William replied. He cast a hand out across his desk, scattering pens and papers and even his own nameplate; all office supplies toppled to the floor. This leg of the meeting wouldn't require any paperwork. Poppy lifted herself up to meet him, capturing him by the hair, pulling him down with her onto the desk. She was determined to make him love this piece of furniture, and she would be willing to meet *as many times as he liked until he was satisfied.*

Now *this* was how you sealed a deal.

CHAPTER FOURTEEN

WILLIAM

S o this is what it felt like to be nervous.

Heart racing, palms tingling, mild lightheadedness. It was a distantly familiar sensation. Once upon a time, when he was younger and greener, William had gotten nerves before presentations—especially ones made to his father. And his father had *insisted* on being present for every one when he was just starting out. Over time, William's anxiety had faded…incessant practice in the form of constant trials-by-fire tended to do that. Years later he had the thought to be thankful to his father for stamping any weakness out of him.

Now he was less than thankful. The weakness hadn't been stamped out at all, only buried deep enough that it had taken years to rise back to the surface and overwhelm him at this singularly inopportune moment.

He stood at the dead center of the room before a group of prospective clients. They all watched him raptly, ready to be impressed. *This* was William Jameson after all, CEO of Jameson Ad Agency, and he was teaming up with his younger brother to deliver a "pitch to end all pitches" for their jewelry company.

At least, that was how Eddie had pre-pitched it to them. "Believe me, every single one of you is going to want to be there for this," he had hyped over drinks a week ago. "And everyone who's in the room the day William pitches is going to be an integral part of the campaign...but I can't say anymore," he had concluded mysteriously, when everyone present had clamored to know exactly that: *more.*

William had to hand it to Eddie: he knew how to generate almost obsessive interest in a project. Now every hungry eye was trained on him, and he was meant to deliver.

Poppy stood in the back of the room, slender arms folded neatly over her chest. Every time William's eyes alighted on her, she nodded encouragingly; he suspected she didn't realize she was doing it. He had asked her to come along today for support, an unusual request for a pitch, but she had agreed on the spot.

Eddie stood politely off to the side, shuffling through his materials and occasionally conversing with the camera operator. "...and so when creating a viral video, the most important thing to understand is that your video has *not* generated the views necessary to make it a viral commodity at the outset," William heard himself saying. His assertion was met with agreeing nods from the potential clients. "If you'll take a look at our associate, Hank, over there beside Eddie—" Eddie waved to attract their attention. "—you will see that while he is a credentialed cameraman hired specifically for this project, he'll be filming with a smartphone. A lower-resolution video taken by expert hands will give the campaign the level of professionalism you have come to expect from Jameson, all while maintaining something other jewelry campaigns never achieve: authenticity. Hank, do you mind switching the camera on now?"

Hank nodded and flipped his phone around. The clientele murmured amongst themselves. "Mr. Jameson, forgive me, but we all know what a viral video is," one of the suits in front said. "Whatever you're leading up to, I must admit it sounds appealing. In fact, it sounds like exactly the sort of thing our company is looking for with its next campaign. But how can you give us your guarantee, as an ad man, that such a strategy would be effective?"

William barely registered the question. His eyes were locked on Poppy. She shifted beneath the weight of his look, blushed and smiled, before trying in vain to nod his attention away from her. Several others had turned to look at her now. "It's important that improvisation play a part in the creation of any viral video," William said. "Poppy, will you join me up here please?"

All heads turned toward the back of the room. Poppy blinked, her green eyes looking even more enormous than usual. She hesitated only a moment, then detached from the wall to join him. "When you said you needed support..." she began, before cutting herself off with a gasp as William dropped to one knee. Her hand flew to her mouth.

"Poppy," William began. "Thank you for your help with this demonstration. I know you weren't expecting it. Can you confirm to the people in the room that your surprise is authentic?"

Poppy nodded wordlessly.

"Can you confirm that neither of us rehearsed this?" He had been in control of his voice until that moment; now he could hear his own heart climbing into it, threatening to choke him off. He was more nervous than he could ever remember being in his life. Even his first presentation for the agency paled in comparison to this.

Poppy nodded.

William drew a small box out of his pocket. "And can… *will* you concede that despite any of the differences we may have come up against in the past, there is no more powerful partnership than the one you and I have already begun to forge together?"

"Conceding isn't something I ever imagined myself doing in *this* scenario," Poppy said wryly. Laughter filled the room, but everyone seemed to be holding their breath. William took her slender hand in his; he popped open the ring box. A dazzling white diamond winked and flashed in the light of the sun streaming in through the boardroom window. It was a radiant gem, perfectly cut to nestle at the center of the gold flower that acted as the ring's setting. Poppy made a small noise as she beheld it for the first time.

"Poppy Hanniford, will you marry me?"

She couldn't hold it together any longer. With an ecstatic sob, Poppy fell to her knees and hugged William, nearly knocking the engagement ring out of his hand. *"Yes!"* she cried.

Everyone in the boardroom was on their feet suddenly and unable to contain their excitement. William pulled back from

Poppy and swiped a thumb across her cheek, banishing her tears of joys. Their eyes met, and for now, there was nothing more they could express to one another in words. He helped her to her feet and slipped the ring on her finger.

"Rhett Butler, eat your heart out," William muttered as he pulled her in.

"Rhett *who?*" Poppy agreed. Their lips met, and William dipped her in his arms. The boardroom receded around them, until all he was aware of was how bright her laugh tasted and how perfectly she filled his embrace. Distantly, he heard Eddie's voice say:

"Turn the camera off, Hank. I think we all got what we need here."

END OF THE BILLIONAIRE'S SEXY RIVAL

JAMESON BROTHERS BOOK THREE

PS: Want to meet a handsome stranger? Keep reading for an exclusive extract from The Sheikh's Fake Fiancée.

THANK YOU!

Thank you so much for purchasing my book. It's hard for me to put into words how much I appreciate my readers. If you enjoyed this book, please remember to leave a review. Reviews are crucial for an author's success and I would greatly appreciate it if you took the time to review the book. I love hearing from you!

If you enjoyed this book please leave a review at:
LeslieNorthBooks.com

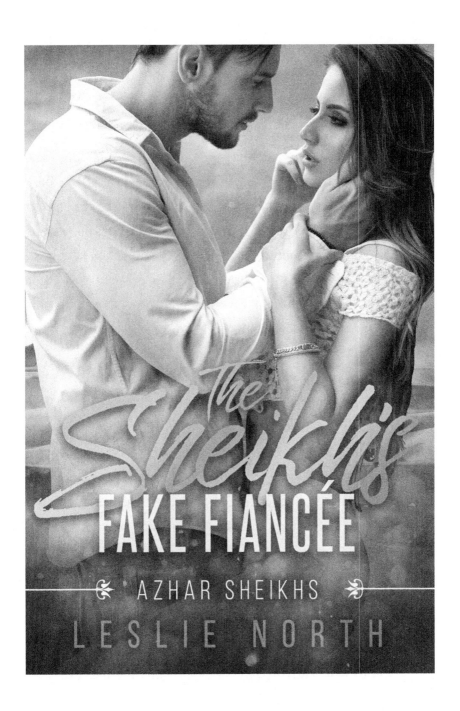

The Sheikh's

FAKE FIANCÉE

❦ AZHAR SHEIKHS ❧

LESLIE NORTH

BLURB

After losing her parents, American artist Elena set out on a trip around the world. Now, in the sultry heat of the Middle East, she's having a hard time imagining returning to real life back home. But with half of her vacation still ahead of her, she and her friend are packed and ready to move onto their next destination when a chance encounter changes everything. A handsome stranger with a devilish grin catches Elena's eye, but how could she know that an innocent favor is about to change her life forever.

Asim always relies on his intuition...with business and with women. Along with his brothers, he works hard to keep their company so profitable, but he prefers to live in the moment. With pressure mounting from his mother to settle down and marry a family friend, Asim needs an escape. He's enchanted by the beguiling American beauty he sees at the café, and she couldn't have come along at a better time. But when he asks her to be his fake fiancée, he never could have known she would change his life forever.

The two waste no time coming together, but when the spontaneity wears off and Elena learns of an unexpected complication, will Asim be ready to face the future?

Grab your copy of The Sheikh's Fake Fiancée at
www.LeslieNorthBooks.com

EXCERPT

Elena sipped at the Turkish coffee, grimacing at the strange bitter flavor that, no matter how many times she ordered it in fumbling Arabic, just didn't taste any better than the first twenty times.

She swallowed it down anyway—*it'll get easier; it's part of the experience*—and sighed happily, enjoying the warm breeze caressing her on the balcony. This was their last morning in Beirut, Lebanon, before she and her friend Aubrey gallivanted onward to Europe. After six weeks on the road, backpacking and sightseeing and gawking and giggling, she found it hard to accept the fact that their trip was halfway over.

Which meant real life loomed just around the corner.

She brought the cup to her mouth again to take a sip but thought better of it. She smiled out at the azure Mediterranean Sea, watching the bustle and clamor of the street below. Cars honked, people filled the sidewalks, and street vendors proffered strange sacks in harsh voices. Gorgeous women strutted in high fashion, oversized sunglasses complementing inky black tresses. She had to pinch herself sometimes to remind herself this was real.

Her parents would have been thrilled to know she'd made it this far. To *Lebanon,* of all places. The Middle East, the farthest from home she'd ever ventured. Her heart tightened in the way it always did when reflecting on accomplishments since her parents' passing, a mixture of pride and sadness. If only they could see her. Good lord, would they be proud of her. A fresh college grad, seeing the world. Less than two months away from taking the leap into trying to make it on her own as an artist.

"Hey, girl." Aubrey's voice cut through Elena's reverie. She turned to greet her friend, pushing aside the diaphanous drapes lining the balcony door to step inside.

"So, it turns out checkout is in half an hour," Aubrey said, flopping onto the skinny twin bed. Elena set her coffee down on the small dresser by the balcony door. "Leaving here at noon was apparently a pipe dream. The sign on the reception desk made it sound like there were stern consequences for overstaying our reservation. Or maybe it was just a bad translation."

"Shit." Elena surveyed the explosion of clothes, the still-wet towel hanging on the back of the bathroom door.

"Yeah. We better get a move on." Aubrey let out a long sigh. "Although we could always reserve an extra night here…"

Elena tutted. "No can do. We have a schedule to maintain." She tapped an imaginary watch on her wrist. Who knew where they'd be if it weren't for her rigid punctuality. If left to her own devices, Aubrey would probably still be in Jordan, lurking around the haunting caverns and monoliths of Petra.

"I know, I know." Aubrey sighed, rolling onto her side. "But seriously, not even an extra day?"

Elena leveled her with a look. "We paid for a ferry to Cyprus tonight."

"You're right." Aubrey groaned, rolling off the bed. "Time to fill up Ol' Lumpy."

Elena smirked at the pet name for her backpack her friend

had coined during their trip. The two made excellent travel partners, which didn't surprise her because they'd also been excellent roommates in college. They'd been random roommates their freshman year, hit it off like long-lost twins, and had been inseparable ever since. If they had shared the same major, that would have been the only thing to make college better—but Aubrey's degree in history only matched Elena's major in fine arts in their mutual appreciation for very old art.

Elena gathered the loose sheets of paper from the small desk near the balcony door, the sketches she'd started outlining over the course of their trip. It seemed every other turn presented her with a new sight, a new moment, a new hue to capture. She'd have enough painting material for a decade after this trip—and maybe, just maybe, it would turn into a lucrative series down the road. The only thing urging her homeward was the itchy desire to feel the acrid sting of paint thinner in the air as she started with a blank canvas.

If only there'd been a way to fit her easel, five canvases, and the entirety of her oil paint collection in this twenty-liter backpack. *Like airport security would have let you through with the paint thinner.*

"Elena, do you want these?" Aubrey held up a handful of postcards from the nightstand between the two twin beds. Elena squinted, recognizing them as the postcards she'd bought to write to her parents.

"Yes, I need those!" She leaned forward to grab them, flipping one over to confirm the letter she'd begun.

Dear Mom & Pops,

Sometimes, it seems like writing these letters means I could actually send them, and maybe you'd receive them. Like any other traveling daughter experiencing the world. But I know when I get home you won't be there. You'd think after three years I'd have gotten used to this a little bit more.

The postcard wasn't finished, but that could be taken care of later, during their boat ride to the island. Writing letters she'd never send had been an unexpected project during the trip—somehow a therapy and a memento at the same time. They didn't make her as sad as she might have thought. Rather, it made her feel even closer to them, especially as she embarked upon such new adventures as a freshly minted college graduate.

Grab your copy of The Sheikh's Fake Fiancée from www.LeslieNorthBooks.com

Printed in Great Britain
by Amazon

35791827R00086